BOUND

THE CURSE TRILOGY BOOK 2

NICOLE MARSH
CASSY JAMES

Copyright © 2020 by Nicole Marsh & Cassy James. All rights reserved.

Cover Art by Spellbinding Designs

No part of this book may be reproduced in any form or by any electronic or mechanical means, including information storage and retrieval systems, without written permission from the author, except for the use of brief quotations in a book review. This is a work of fiction. Names, characters, businesses, places, events, and incidents are either the product of the author's imagination or used simply for the purpose of furthering the storyline and do not represent the institutions or places of business in any way. Any resemblance to actual persons, living or dead, or actual events is purely coincidental or used for fictional purposes.

This book is the continuation of a series and cannot be read as a standalone. It does contain some material that may be triggering to some readers.

If you have not read the first book in the series:
Cursed: The Curse Trilogy Book 1
It can be found at: www.books2read.com/TCT1

MIRABELLA LOVE

Last month my mom went all "Yer a Wizard, Harry." Except her exact words were "You're a Witch, Mira." Same, diff.

Next thing I know, my spare grandmother pops out of the woodwork and insinuates I'm essential to breaking a curse that no one seems to believe in. Nothing is ever as simple as finding a magical cure to save humanity though.

First, I have to pass my witches exams. Then, the elders will attempt to help me save my town. On top of everything else, Vlad decides to channel his inner Houdini and pulls a disappearing act.

Now I'm juggling my missing rude, but hot ex-best friend (who's now kind of my boyfriend), practicing magic, and holding down a full-time job with a boss I think is crushing on me.

No pressure, right?

CONTENTS

1.	The Mistake	1
2.	The Surprise	12
3.	The Dinner	27
4.	The Daily	38
5.	The Bully	51
6.	The Canadian	61
7.	The Potion	64
8.	The Warning	77
9.	The Toad	83
10.	The Gift	91
11.	The Offer	101
12.	The Countdown	111
13.	The Exam	120
14.	The Sabotage	130
15.	The Celebration	137
16.	The Return	148
17.	The Savior	155
18.	The Recovery	163
19.	The Intel	172
20.	The Roadtrip	177
21.	The Room	185
22.	The Spring	195
23.	The Threat	206
24.	The Reveal	216
25.	The Portal	226
26.	The City	233

Interested in news about books by Nicole Marsh?	243
Interested in news about books by Cassy James?	245
Books by Nicole Marsh	247
Books by Cassy James	249

1

THE MISTAKE

Mirabella

"One pinch of blan-something leaves," I mutter to myself, reading the instructions from a potion's manual. Pulling the jar of blan... something leaves closer, I read the name off the front to confirm the ingredient. Blancara leaves. I repeat the words a few times, trying to pronounce it correctly, then grab what I estimate to be a pinch. Dropping the leaves into my cauldron with one hand, I cross the fingers on my other, hoping the spell works.

A small popping noise echoes across the chamber.

Then, nothing.

I stir a few more times, eyes widening as the golden colored liquid transitions to a murky green. This is it! I'm mastering my first potion! I clap my hands together giddily, then pull my potions manual towards me to quadruple check I haven't missed any steps.

I'm mentally checking off each direction while I read, muttering the words as my finger traces them down the page. My distraction keeps me from noticing the green smoke billowing out of the cauldron.

A slight tickle hits my throat and I cough lightly. The movement provides only a brief reprieve from the itchy feeling crawling through my esophagus. Next thing I know, it feels like I've swallowed a furball. I clear my throat twice, but the feeling only intensifies.

Suddenly, I can't breathe. I'm gasping for air through the thick feeling clogging my throat. I begin choking and coughing, attempting to clear my airway and rid myself of the awful sensation.

My eyes are watering from the fit. I know I need to find some water, but I can't see clearly. When I'm finally able to open my eyes fully, between gasps for breath, I intend to look for said water, but inhale sharply at the scene before me instead.

Green smoke is seeping out of the cauldron at a rapid pace, already covering the ground with a murky layer. It's swirling around my ankles as it fills the room.

I desperately flip through the pages of my manual, looking for anything that can help me undo... whatever I did. Covering my mouth with my fist, I cough into it and frantically wave my arm in the air near the cauldron. I'm trying to dissipate some of the green smoke oozing into the room while my eyes rapidly skim potion names.

I'm panicking by the time the smoke reaches my knees with no sign of letting up. My lungs are screaming for air, and my eyes water, as the green fog becomes a thick wall, coating every surface in the room, with no pause in sight.

Abandoning my attempts to fix the problem I've created, I push through the green-tinged air blindly, searching for the wooden door nearby. I clutch my manual to my chest with my left hand, sliding my right along the wall.

Smiling in victory once my hand reaches the cool metal handle, I press down and open the door just enough for me to slip out, and quickly exit the room. Despite my hasty escape, the victorious feeling is short lived.

As I slam the door shut behind me, leaning against it to ensure it closes fully, I resume hacking up a lung. A puff of green smoke appears in the air by my face at the tail end of the coughing fit and my eyes widen in shock.

Did I swallow some of the smoke or is this going to become a permanent issue?

Testing my lungs, I huff out a few more breaths, thankful when the air appears to be clear. When I'm finally able to catch my breath, and rid myself of the fear of permanent green puff exhales, disappointment seeps deep into my bones.

I didn't realize this witch thing would be so hard. When my mom showed me our witching chamber a month ago, on my eighteenth birthday, I was filled with wonder and excitement. *I'm a witch! A real witch!* Played on repeat in my mind.

But little did I know, being a witch is actually super difficult.

Silly, naïve, newly eighteen-year old me, thought convincing the shifter council to let me go would be the biggest challenge I would face. Then, my grandmother appeared and determined it's a priority for me to earn my witching license as soon as possible. Since then, I've been plugging away, trying to channel a talent that is supposedly innate—brewing potions—but the more I try, the more I think maybe the witch gene skipped a generation. Now, wiser, eighteen years and one month old me is realizing: maybe I'm not cut out for this.

Interrupting my own morose thoughts, I shove off the door and head to the stone steps leading into my parent's room. I need to find my mom so she can help me clear out the chaos that I unintentionally caused.

I trudge upstairs, taking my time and holding the wall out of caution. Last week I slipped and tumbled down a fair portion of our secret passageway. It was a hard lesson in caution. Literally. The secret stone of my home is very unforgiving to land on.

After distractedly winding my way through the hall, I emerge into my parents' bedroom and replace the bookshelf. Wandering around the top floor, I quickly realize it's empty and jog downstairs, hoping my parents are in the kitchen.

I barrel through the doorway only to pull up short

when I realize my parents and the Morts are sitting at the table in the kitchen nook and look to be having a deep, serious conversation.

Mr. Mort's eyes slide to me then back to my dad and he makes a huge, fake-sounding cough into his fist. Suddenly four pairs of eyes are on me and every face that was serious turns into a beaming smile.

I'm instantly suspicious.

"Are you here about Vlad? Is he back yet?" I demand, skipping pleasantries and delving right into the most important issue.

Tricia slides off the bench and comes to wrap me in a tight hug. "Mira, love. We haven't heard from Vlad yet, but I'm sure we will soon. This is typical of young wolves, to run for a while and blow off steam. There's no reason to worry..." The "Yet" is silent, but I hear the way her sentence lingers as if she left it off at the last second.

I return her squeeze tightly, then step back. "Okay, but will you have him call me as soon as you hear from him?" I ask. My words are more gentle than before, as I consider her tired eyes and messy ponytail.

"Of course, dear. Of course." She pats my shoulder consolingly before moving to slide back into the booth next to her husband. "Are you hungry? You came barreling down here like you were being chased by a rabid raccoon!"

I chuckle before memories of the green smoke sober me. Shuffling my feet, I mutter, "I actually need some help in the witching chamber."

My mom's smile dims immediately. "What is it this time?"

My hackles raise a little at her tone. Normally my parents don't get snippy with me, but I guess the fact that I've flooded the witching chamber, set three curtains on fire with some wayward liquid, and turned the neighbor's cat into a goldfish—all in the past week—has everyone a bit on edge about my current witching abilities.

"I don't think it's TOO big of a deal," I start.

In response to my hedging, the adults immediately stand and briskly head for the entrance of the kitchen that leads to the stairs. I rush forward to catch up, shouting, "We might need some masks or something!"

A chorus of groans erupts down the hall in response.

"I have some supplies in the garage," my dad announces. He separates from the group to grab tools for cleaning up my mess.

Releasing a sigh, I watch my dad round the corner then trail behind the rest of the adults, slowly trudging up the steps. I'm embarrassed about causing such a big issue, again. When I finally place my feet on the top step a couple dozen feet behind everyone else, my dad appears at the bottom of the stairs below. He has some weird cross body backpack strapped across his chest, an icepick, three fire extinguishers, a slew of gas masks, and a canister of glowing liquid.

I let out a deep exhale, bordering on a sigh, waiting to see if he needs help carrying anything. When he reaches the top of the stairs, he pats my shoulder. "You'll get better, kiddo." I'm sure he meant to be reassuring, but the end of his statement comes out like a question.

I ignore the defeat that's bubbling up in my belly and tamp down my distress over sucking so badly at something that's supposed to be in my blood. Pushing all my negative feelings down, I reply, "It just takes time, I know Dad. Can I help you carry anything?"

My dad begins to pull the canister off his body, then appears to second guess his decision. "You know what, kiddo? I think you can just watch this time and help next time." He hands me a mask to soften the blow of his words and then turns to follow the rest of the parents into his bedroom.

Gripping the mask, I follow slowly behind.

Sylvia releases another chuckle, "How long did it take for them to clear out the smoke?"

"Almost five hours," I groan as I swirl my brush across a canvas, blending pink and purple hues until I'm satisfied with the shading.

"And now you're banned from the witching chamber?" She continues.

"Only unsupervised," I mumble. "How did you pass your test? It seems so impossible. I'm pretty sure I'm the worst witch that's ever existed," I gripe.

Sylvia passed her witches exams with flying colors, just last week. This isn't the first time I've asked her how she passed, but she hasn't given me a direct answer. She keeps telling me she can't talk about the specifics. I guess the coven thinks of that as cheating.

"It will come with time," Sylvia reassures me. "I was terrible at first, too. Then one day it clicked and all of my potions started to work properly. The more you concoct, the easier it gets. Cut yourself some slack... you've been at this, what, a week?"

With a sigh, I throw my paintbrush down and stretch my arms above my head. I'm tired of being terrible at potions, but I know Sylvia's right. I need to stop having such a defeatist attitude.

I hear Sylvia slowly pad over to inspect my completed painting. Instead of turning around, I do the same. In the center of the canvas is an onyx black wolf, a wolf I now know to be Vlad, but other than that not much else makes sense. There are dark figures that appear to be floating through the sky on discs, large pink buildings, including a castle with turrets, and an old, cobblestone street running down the center in between.

"Another one with the pink buildings, huh?" Sylvia asks, throwing her arms over my shoulders, sensing my need to change the subject.

"Yeah, I guess so." I respond, still eyeing the canvas.

"Kind of looks like Candy Land, don't you think?" She replies.

Before I can respond, a ringing trills through the air. Glancing around, I spot my cell sitting in the far corner of the studio, on my rack of unpainted canvases. I slip out of Sylvia's arms and dive across the room.

Catching the phone on the last ring, I answer without checking the caller ID. "Hello," I wheeze, breathless from my ninja like moves to reach my phone.

"Hello dear," My grandma's nasally voice states through the receiver.

I ignore the small pang of disappointment I feel when I realize it isn't Vlad and focus my attention on my grandma. "Hey grandma, what's going on? Any luck yet? Do you need me to come over?" I blurt in quick succession.

"Slow down, dear. Slow down. My old lady brain can't handle your barrage of questions. I need them one at a time. To answer the first, I'm calling because I have a surprise for you. Something I think you'll be very excited to... see."

"A surprise for me?" I ask, my tone rising in pitch with my excitement. A small part of my brain is asking, what if she's found Vlad? Enthusiasm takes over as I continue, "I have Sylvia with me, should we head over right now?"

I hear the smile in my grandma's voice, even though her tone remains basically the same. "No, no. Not tonight. It won't arrive until tomorrow. How about you come over around eleven?"

What. If. It's. Vlad?

Shoving the thought away, I reply, "Yes. I'll see you at eleven."

"Okay dear. Try to get some decent sleep tonight

and I'll see you in the morning. I think you'll be very appreciative for what I have in store."

"Thanks Grandma. See you tomorrow!" I exclaim, my brain already creating a countdown until eleven am the following day, when I'll hopefully reunite with Vlad.

After we hang up, Sylvia quirks a brow at me. "Grams has a surprise for you?"

Grinning from ear to ear, I nod. "That's why she called. I don't want to get my hopes up, but it has to be Vlad, right? Or at least related to Vlad? I'm trying not to set myself up for disappointment, but I'm hoping it is," I admit, my smile dropping into a frown. Then I add, "There has to be some news by now... we've been searching for an entire month."

Sylvia runs her hands through her short, lime-green hair and purses her lips. "Well, I can't tell you what your gram's surprise is, but I'm sure even if it isn't Vlad, you'll appreciate whatever she has in store. She's a bit of a kook, but a wise kook, ya know?"

I nod at her assessment. Then, I shudder thinking of our strange encounter with my grandmother just a few days prior.

It was her first time meeting any of my friends, besides Vlad. My grandma was immediately obsessed with Sylvia's short green locks. She essentially interrogated her about potions, attempting to identify how she created such a vibrant color. My grandmother absolutely refused to believe there was any other way to create such a look.

After the intensive round of questioning, she forced Sylvia onto the living room to lay head to head. Then, my grandma proceeded to drape Sylvia's hair over her own while I took photos, so she could "see what it would look like".

The fact that Sylvia still thinks she's wise after all that is, frankly, a bit astounding.

Sylvia interrupts my thoughts, "How about we rent that new Vampire movie? We can get some ice cream and extra butter popcorn. It will be a good distraction."

A small trickle of ice-cold fear runs down my back. "... Vampires don't exist, right? Those are still a myth?" I ask tentatively.

Sylvia laughs, her entire face scrunching with the force of her smile and her hands clutching her belly with her mirth. When she finally calms down, she wipes the corners of her eyes and replies, "As far as I know, Hollywood made them up to sell gory movies and sappy love stories."

I tame my sigh of relief, to prevent another laughing fit at my expense. In my defense, I didn't believe potion-brewing witches or wolf shifters existed either. Following their recent discovery, I think anything could be possible. And blood-sucking vampires are more terrifying, but not that far of a stretch from the others.

Forcing my attention back to Sylvia, I say, "I think a movie night is exactly what we need."

2

THE SURPRISE

Mirabella

My alarm blares jarringly into the morning air. Pivoting around on my vanity chair, I dash across the room to shut it off. Anxious excitement twisted through my chest all night, and I barely slept as a result. I've been awake for hours, sketching in a notepad and waiting for my alarm. Now, I can finally prepare for my day. Then, in a few short hours, I'll head to my grandmother's.

Eleven cannot come soon enough.

I force myself to shower leisurely, instead of conducting the quick rinse my mind is urging. When I emerge from the steamy room, pruney and clean, I return to my vanity and slowly brush out my long, blonde hair. I deliberately apply mascara to the lashes surrounding my pale gray eyes at a steady pace, then swipe-on a lightly tinted gloss.

Acting like I possess patience, I peruse my wardrobe, selecting a light blue summer dress with flutter sleeves. I take my time buckling my shoes and finding a purse, shoveling my belongings inside.

I make myself slowly walk down the stairs, taking each step one at a time, instead of bounding down like I want to. Rounding the corner into the kitchen, I grab a banana then finally allow myself to check to time.

10:20.

It's about a fifteen-minute drive to grandma's house, meaning it's still too early to head over. Unless... I drive a little slower. I need to be cautious about any wildlife that may run into the road unprovoked or any stray wolves possibly roaming the woods near my grandmother's.

Given the need to drive slower, for safety, it would be incredibly reasonable to leave now and ensure I'm not late. There's nothing more impolite than being late, I reason as I exit my house and stride to my Prius.

Slowly, cautiously, I back down the steep drive and turn onto the Main Road. More quickly than expected, I'm on the packed dirt leading to my grandma's house. Within minutes, I'm sitting outside her tiny cottage, nestled in the tree and slightly hidden by the foliage.

Tapping my fingers on the steering wheel, I eye the clock on my dash.

10:32.

Am I unreasonably early?

On the one hand, if you're not early, technically

you're late. On the other, there is such a thing as too early.

I stare at the time, warring with indecision, until a flash of movement from my grandmother's porch captures my attention. Glancing up, I spot her dramatically waving in my direction. Once our gazes connect, she gestures for me to come inside.

Hopping out of the car, I jog to the front steps. "Hey grandma, sorry I'm early." I pause, deciding whether I should make up an excuse.

My brain is consumed with thoughts of Vlad, making it difficult to think of anything else, including a legitimate reason for my premature arrival. "I thought it would take longer to get here." I finish lamely, sticking with the half-truth I used on myself.

"It's okay, Dear. Your surprise is ready now, anyway. Come in, come in."

Butterflies flutter in my belly as I cross the threshold. I follow closely on my grandmother's heels. Well, as close as possible, while I avoid the swishing fabric of her navy colored robes as they billow behind her.

We barely make it five steps before I'm unable to contain my excitement any longer. "Is it the tracking spell? Have you found…?" I trail off as my grandmother stops suddenly.

My eyes flit to a tall guy with a slim build and overly gelled blonde hair as he rises from the couch in the living room. I scan him briefly, then return my gaze to my grandmother, hoping he's here with information on Vlad.

"Mira, this is Leif," my grandma states. She gestures towards the guy, a beaming smile on her face.

"A pleasure to meet you," Leif states in a surprisingly deep voice with a light accent that I can't quite identify.

He takes a step closer and proffers his hand for a handshake. I bury my disappointment over the fact that he isn't Vlad and take his hand. A small shock of electricity travels between us. My eyes flash upwards to meet the guy's muddy gaze, but he doesn't appear to notice.

Leif continues to grasp my palm for a few beats longer than appropriate. I delicately slip my smaller hand from his and then face my grandmother, waiting for her to explain my 'surprise'.

In her usual fashion, she doesn't. Grandma never lets a moment to tell a lengthy story while sipping tea pass her by.

"Why don't you two sit down and get comfortable? I'll make us some refreshments before we chat." she offers, instead.

As she putters away, I gingerly sit on the floral couch Vlad and I normally share, across from Leif. I watch from underneath my lashes as he gracefully folds his long limbs back onto the cushion. Avoiding his gaze, I direct my attention downwards to my lap, plucking at an imaginary ball of lint before folding my hands together. A ticking from one of the eclectic items on my grandma's shelves penetrates the silence.

Leif clears his throat twice, then breaks the silence when he asks, "You're a Spells too then, eh?"

His question is a bit odd, referring to my grandmother's last name. Well, and my mother's maiden name. "Technically, I'm a Love." I say with a small grin. He nods slightly and I engage, out of courtesy, if nothing else. "And you are?"

Leif smiles, allowing the expression to take over his entire face. His thin lips spread even thinner with the movement and reveal a set of straight, blunt teeth. His eyes crinkle at the corners, making me think he's a tad older than I originally expected, which was about my age. "I'm Leif Golden," he replies, a hint of his unidentifiable accent peeking through his words once more.

I nod politely, as his name means nothing to me. His smile loosens a bit at my reaction, but remains plastered on his face until my grandmother returns with her tray.

Leif hops from the couch and takes two long strides forward, murmuring, "Allow me."

He takes the dish from my grandmother and ushers her towards her armchair off to the side. He delicately places the loaded tray on the coffee table and proceeds to pour three cups of tea, offering the first to my grandmother with a "Milady".

I watch in shock as a bright pink blush flares across my grandmother's cheeks.

Interesting.

Leif offers me a cup next. I lean forward, briefly brushing his fingers with mine and receiving another minor shock as the cup exchanges hands. I belatedly murmur, "Thank you." Then I settle against the back of the couch, avoiding Leif's probing gaze, and focusing on my grandmother, awaiting her explanation.

She sips her tea and releases a soft sigh. She opens her mouth as if to speak and at the last second, changes her mind. Instead, she sets her tea onto the side table and heaves herself out of her chair to place a few cookies from the tea tray onto a napkin.

I stifle a groan of exasperation, already knowing if I try to rush her, my grandmother will take even longer to tell her story. As a distraction, I swirl my tea around its cup before taking a small sip. The cinnamon flavored liquid warms my insides, and I find myself relaxing slightly into the couch.

During my next, larger sip, my grandmother speaks. I almost spit the liquid out in surprise. My eyes water as I force my throat to swallow and contain my coughs to keep from interrupting her, now that she's begun.

"Leif is here from the Canadian Coven. He is the son of my contact and has graciously agreed to help you study for your witches exams," my grandmother states, looking at me with a pleased expression.

Leif is Canadian. That explains the tinge of an accent I detected earlier. I mull the rest of my grandmother's statement over, a question forming as I contemplate her words. Cocking my head to the side as I scan Leif's face, I ask, "Well, thank you for traveling all this way. Forgive my impoliteness, but why do you want to help me?"

Leif's large smile steals across his face again, "Well, partially to repay a favor from your family from years prior. Although I'm not here just to help you learn. Any issue affecting the supernatural world, such as the one with the shifter population, is a concern for everyone. My coven is interested in finding more information about what is happening and why."

"So, are you here to train or investigate?" I question, trying to keep my tone light. Despite his casual demeanor, Leif's explanation seems suspicious to me. When my grandmother went for help, her contact turned her away claiming I would need to pass my witches exams first. Then they send someone to Florence to "help"?

"Well, both." Leif replies, sounding almost apologetic. "You couldn't travel to us for assistance without passing your witches exams, but my father felt we may be able to help you pass regardless."

I consider his words and decide I was being too defensive. It makes sense for Leif's coven to send someone here, since I'm not yet able to go there, right? His coven appears to be invested in helping and I'm attempting to create nefarious intentions that don't exist, instead of appreciating their offer.

With my mind feeling more settled, I smile slightly. "Well, thank you again. When can we get started?"

"Ahh, not so fast, Mira Dear." My grandmother states. "Leif traveled quite some distance and just recently arrived. He needs a chance to settle in, maybe even get a feel for the town, before being forced into potion brewing." Although her reprimand is a bit harsh, my grandma offers a smile when she's done speaking to soften the blow.

Passing my witches exams puts me one step closer to curing the wolves, and hopefully finding Vlad. I'm eager to start as quickly as possible and her words deflate the small feeling of hope that had begun to well.

"I know you miss Vlad, dear. It's only been a week since he ran off with those wolves and I'm sure he's safe. We'll find a way to bring him back soon," my grandma's quiet words startle me from my thoughts.

They provide little comfort, but I offer her a small smile, anyway. "Thanks, grandma." Facing Leif, I force a brighter tone, "After my shift at the Daily, would you like me to show you around Downtown? We could walk the shops and eat some ice cream."

"I would quite like that," Leif replies in his lightly accented tone. He's wearing a polite smile, but has an odd twinkle in his eye. Like he and my grandmother are in on a joke I haven't been made aware of, yet.

Ignoring the feeling of being left out, I focus my gaze on my remaining tea. The silence lingers until the lack of noise is stifling. I'm ready to go home, but I'm not sure how to politely excuse myself after less than half an hour. Neither Leif, nor my grandma, seem as uncomfortable by the silence as I am. In fact, Leif has nestled back into his couch, half-lounging against the cushions as he sips his tea.

My eyes slide up his legs, crossed at the ankle and half covered by the coffee table, all the way up his lanky form to observe his relaxed face. Leif has a broad, slightly upturned nose, wide almond shaped eyes, thin lips with a slightly narrowed jaw, all topped with his gelled hair. Separately his features would not be deemed attractive, but together they give him an almost exotic look, making me wonder about his heritage. His hair is almost the same color as mine, about one shade darker, and his stature is quite large, making me think of a Viking.

I smile at the thought of Leif with a Viking braid, carrying an axe. A second later, I realize a smile has formed across Leif's face in response. He's been watching me examine him.

A flush much worse than my grandmother's blooms on my face, and I quickly return my gaze to the teacup resting in my lap. Focusing on the liquid, I bring the ceramic to my lips and take another sip. The silence continues on as I drink.

Once my cup is empty, the room becomes almost unbearable. Clearing my throat, I ask Leif, "So... where are you staying? In town?"

"Oh, no. I'll stay here with Molly. Of course," Leif replies, the annunciation of his vowels highlighting his Canadian accent. He aims a smile towards my grandmother at the end of his statement.

She returns the look endearingly, as if he's her

long-lost grandson, and I wonder how long they've known each other. I debate asking, but ultimately decide against it. Neither of them speaks again, and the room falls back into silence.

I'm beginning to wonder if I've always been so awkward or if it's just something about this situation. There isn't anything wrong with Leif, at least not that I can tell, and I appreciate that he's come all this way to help me, but his presence puts me on edge.

I tentatively rise from the couch and place my teacup back on the tray. "I think I should head back to my house," I tell my grandmother. "I need to get a few things ready for work tomorrow. After my shift, I'll pick up Leif and we can see downtown."

"Okay Dear, thank you for coming by on short notice," she replies, before taking another sip of her tea and exhaling a small sigh. "We'll see you tomorrow."

Leif and my grandmother rise from the couch in sync and follow me to the door, as if they're co-hosts. I hug my grandma goodbye and give Leif a weird wave. Then I dash out the door and down the steps to my car.

I hop in before glancing back towards the cottage. My grandma and Leif are still standing on the steps waving at me. Brushing off all the strangeness of the visit, I fling a quick wave out my window, and reverse towards the dirt road.

The second my tires hit the Main Road, I call Sylvia. Thankfully, she answers on the second ring, her voice singsonging words through my car stereo, "Was it Vlad? Are the lovebirds back together again?"

Sighing, I reply, "No. It was some guy named Leif. He's from the Canadian Coven, I guess…"

A shriek interrupts before I can finish my sentence, "Leif Who?!? Leif Who?"

"Uhm Leif Golden." I say hesitantly, confused by her sudden shouting.

A loud fangirl type scream fills my ears and I wince. Sylvia starts speaking excitedly, the words spilling out of the speakers so fast it takes me a second to decipher them. "Leif Golden? THE Leif Golden? What was he like? Is he handsome? Oh my god, wait. Don't tell me yet, I'm coming over."

The click of the phone echoes through my car as she ends the call. Her excitement fills me with curiosity and I drive home faster than usual. Seconds after I park, I spot a lime green flash jolting down the sidewalk.

Standing next to my car, I wait for Sylvia to hustle up my driveway, watching as her troll green hair whips in the wind created by her speed. She reaches me and immediately begins spewing words between panted breaths. I catch "witching-web", "potions master", and "video blog" before waving my hands in the air to stop her.

"I can't understand what you're saying, psychopath. Let's go inside and get some snacks. You can tell me about him in the studio."

We settle into my studio's oversized leather chairs with a slew of snacks settled between us. "Okay, spill. Who is this Leif guy?" I ask, grabbing a handful of carrots to munch while Sylvia explains.

Her eyes widen. "I can't believe you've never heard of him."

Pointing a finger back at myself, I respond, "New to witching, remember?"

Sylvia nods with two Cheetos sticking out of her mouth while pulling her phone from her back pocket. "Ohmkay, mwell mI'll shmow moo," she mumbles out while crunching on the chips. Placing her phone between us, she types in wwww.foogle.com.

I'm about to remark that she's typed in too many w's. But I swallow my words as a screen pops up. One that I've never seen before. Instead of the traditional Foogle screen, white with a non-descript search bar, the screen is all black with a blue bar to type your questions.

"What is this?" I whisper, as if speaking too loudly will make the website disappear.

"World-wide witching web," Sylvia replies. She doesn't add a "duh" on the end, but her tone implies it should be there. "How do you think we can find information or order supplies? It's not like you can go onto regular Foogle and type in 'Where can I find blancara leaves?'"

I make a mental note to wipe my laptop's internet browser history before Sylvia gets ahold of it. I would never hear the end of it if she saw I had, in fact, typed that question into Foogle. A few days ago, I realized our blancara leaf supply was getting low from all my butchered potion brewing.

"I thought our history and recipes for potions were all in books and potions manuals." I state, wondering about the functions of this "witching web".

"Well, duh. But books are so old school," Sylvia replies. "Almost everything you can find in books is on wwww, well except like really bad stuff. Obviously, no one wants that to be public knowledge."

My mind wanders back to the days Vlad, and I spent at my grandma's house, searching through dusty old texts. We definitely became closer while working together, but it would have been a heck of a lot easier if we had known about the witching web then.

Bringing my thoughts back to the present, I focus on Sylvia's phone. She's logged into a popular video website called MeTube, where people post all types of videos that anyone with an account can view.

She types in 'Leif Golden' and a familiar blonde-haired guy pops up. I release a sharp gasp at the sight. Not only is he on the witching web's MeTube, but he has over five-hundred and fifty thousand followers for his videos.

"Who is this guy?" I whisper, more to myself than to Sylvia.

She smirks at me. "I can't believe you've never heard of him. He creates his own potions all the time and films the process. Then he posts them here for anyone to watch or recreate. Some of them are really dangerous, but he always makes them work. He's basically famous. His Dad is some super important potions master too. People travel from all over the world to get his help with crazy problems."

"Wow." The response barely scratches the surface of the thoughts swirling around my brain. Maybe Leif can find Vlad, cure the wolves and break the curse, if he's as good as Sylvia says he is. A renewed sense of hope wells up inside me.

Sylvia presses play on a video, interrupting my thoughts of Florence and the shifters. Together we watch as Leif pinches and pours ingredients into a giant pewter cauldron, occasionally stirring.

It's kind of freaky comparing the cocky guy in the video, dressed in nice slacks and a button-up, to the much quieter guy at my grandmother's in jeans and a t-shirt. Leif definitely adapts to his environment.

When he's finished brewing, he uses a ladle to pour a scoop of bionic blue potion from the cauldron into a vial. He shows off the jarred liquid, then places it on the table in view of the camera. I admire the potion he was able to whip up with ease. Immediately after the glass jar hits the table, Leif uses the ladle to throw another scoop of the blue liquid onto the ground, right in front of him.

In a puff of smoke, he disappears.

When the video finishes, a half dozen questions fight for my attention. I ask the most pressing, "Do you think other witches will recognize him if we go to Downtown Florence together?"

Sylvia hmms, looking contemplative. After a minute, she shrugs, "It's possible. I mean, he's basically a witch celebrity. Honestly though, they might not connect his face with his name unless you go around yelling, 'Leif Golden'. He's not really known for his distinguished looks, just his potion brewing skills."

The relief her words create is palpable. "I hope you're right," I respond.

The last thing I want is a bunch of kids from school that hate me, swarming Leif and I asking for his autograph as we walk downtown tomorrow.

"If nothing else, he'll at least be able to help you pass your witches exams. Even if you have to fight off hordes of crazed fans," Sylvia says with a wink, anticipating where my mind was headed, without me having to say the thought aloud.

"Let's hope the first part of your statement is true, and the second doesn't happen," I reply with a laugh.

3

THE DINNER

Mirabella

Today marks eight days since Vlad's disappearance into the forest near my grandma's. It's the second Sunday dinner in my entire life that I remember the presence of both our parents, but no Vlad.

I tried to convince Sylvia to stay after she showed me the videos on MeTube, but she adamantly declined. Her excuse was that she needed to go practice a haircut on her mannequin head before she did the same style on a live model at school tomorrow. As much as I want her support, I also don't want her to butcher someone's hair and fail her test. She was able to convince me she wouldn't have enough time to study if she stayed. I finally relented and reluctantly said goodbye an hour before the Morts arrived.

Now, sitting at the dinner table with Vlad's empty

seat beside me, I wish I would've pushed a little harder for Sylvia to keep me company. The usual chatter seems muted compared to its normal vibrancy. The Morts try to retain their typically upbeat personalities, while my parents carry the majority of the conversation.

I can tell Tricia tried to hide the bags under her eyes with concealer, but she looks exhausted. Tonight, her normally silky hair looks greasy and neglected. Even the hug she gave me when she walked in the front door, was more like being held by a limp noodle, than her normal tight squeeze.

I think everyone is trying to keep up the routine, as if the Morts missing a Sunday dinner is admitting that Vlad is missing and no one knows where he went or if he'll be back.

I'm shaken from my thoughts when I suddenly become the focus of everyone's gaze. "Uhm, sorry. I missed the question…" I state timidly.

My dad lets out a more-mild-than-usual chuckle, then throws me a lifeline, "Your mom asked what your grandma wanted to see you about today."

The question takes me aback momentarily. My mom hasn't exactly said anything against me hanging out with my grandma, her "dead" mother, but she also hasn't encouraged me to talk about what we do together. After I overcome my shock, I appreciate my mom's interest in my day, despite the fact that she hasn't mended her relationship with her mother, and may never do so.

I hesitate a brief second then respond, "Oh, she said she had a surprise for me. I was hoping it would be related to a potion she's brewing to find..." My eyes slide to the Morts briefly. "A mall that sells better socks," I finish lamely, not wanting to bring up the topic we've all been avoiding.

"And was she able to find... the mall with the socks?" My dad asks, his brow furrowed quizzically.

"Uhm, no. Well, I'm not sure," I backtrack. "At least that's not why she called me to come over today. She had a guy there. His name is Leif. Leif Golden. Grandma said he came here on behalf of the Canadian Coven to help me pass my witches exams."

It seems like my words cause all the adults at the table to exchange a glance I can't interpret. After their silent communication, four pairs of eyes come back to rest on my face.

"Well, sweetie." Tricia begins cautiously, "It's great for the Canadian Coven to offer some assistance, but just... be cautious of this Leif. The Canadian Coven..." She pauses, looking contemplative. Her fingers tap against the table as she considers her words, finally continuing with pursed lips, "Well they're not known to always follow the rules."

"Are you saying they're dangerous?" I ask, confused by her wary tone.

"No, no, nothing that dramatic, Mira.' My mom chimes in, a smile plastered to her face. "They're just a different coven, in a different place, with different rules. That's all. Every coven is different, and you should always be mindful when interacting with witches from different places. We just wanted to make sure you remembered to follow the guiding principles of our coven, even if Leif's does things a bit differently. That's all."

"I'm sure he'll be a great instructor and help you pass your witches exams in no time." My dad tacks on, his tone upbeat.

"Oh, of course," my mom adds on. "I'm sorry Mira, I wasn't trying to sound discouraging." Her tone is contrite, and she continues to explain, "We all want you to pass your witches exams, as soon as possible. Then you can start practicing with the coven. I think our overprotective mom instincts were just kicking in," she says with a self-deprecating laugh and a look at Tricia.

Mr. Mort has remained silent. I look to him to see if he has any advice. He takes a sip of water, but right before I look away, he offers me a wink over the top of his glass. Maybe he thinks the other adults are being too dramatic after all.

"Well, thank you for the advice. I'll keep it in mind when working with Leif. I trust your instincts and won't keep brewing with him if it seems like he's dangerous or trying to get me to do something I know I shouldn't. I just hope he can help... I want to start working with the coven too." I flash a smile to everyone seated at the table, hoping it helps smooth over the awkwardness Leif's name brought to our dinner.

The adults exchange one last look, then everyone

turns back to their plates to eat without another word about the Canadian Coven or Leif. Silverware scrapes against the plates in the ensuing silence. A quiet conversation begins between my parents and the Morts, but is unable to hold my attention.

Instead, my gaze continues to drift to the empty chair next to me, which is serving as a constant reminder that Vlad is missing. The irony doesn't escape me. I used to wish Vlad would not show up to Sunday dinner, even just once, as a reprieve from his bullying antics. And now that he's gone, I just wish he was in his chair, even if he threw another soda in my lap, like he used to love doing.

Jacob comes into the dining room and clears the last round of plates, but we all remain seated as if unsure what to do next. After a few beats, my mom abruptly stands up from her chair, "Tricia, Bart, would you like to join us for coffee and desert in the parlor?"

"That sounds lovely," Tricia agrees quietly.

My dad and Bart nod as well, and chairs begin to slide across the floor as the adults stand and file from the room. Normally, Vlad and I would also be obligated to join the coffee and dessert party.

Even when we weren't on speaking terms, we would sit on opposite sides of the room and exchange glares while chatting with everyone else. Tonight, however, I excuse myself and head upstairs to my room.

. . .

I close my bedroom door quietly behind me and slip out of my summer dress into some loose sweats. Grabbing my laptop, I plop onto my bed. I lean against the wall behind my bed, propping myself up with a wall of pillows. Setting my computer on my lap, I type in the address to search the world-wide witching web.

When the same homepage from Sylvia's phone pops up on my screen, I let out a small squeal of excitement. It's real! Even though I just experienced it earlier, in the back of my mind I felt like Sylvia was messing with me. So much has changed since my eighteenth birthday, I'm still not used to this potion, or witches, business. Every time someone mentions witches or magic, it partially feels like they're playing an elaborate prank.

After the page loads, I stare at the screen. I type a few words into the search bar, then delete them. Repeating this process several times before I finally decide where to start. Clicking on the search bar again, I type "The Curse Florence OR".

As much as I want to look for tracking spells and find Vlad, if for no other reason than to scream at him for disappearing without a trace... There are bigger, more important issues at hand. Like the fates of half of our town.

My search pulls up one link with an article. With crossed fingers, I double-click my mousepad and pull it up, hoping it contains at least some of the answers I need.

Skimming the words on the page, disappointment

blooms in my chest. It's literally just an article outlining the legend of Florence. It contains no more information than the children's tale explaining why the Main Road separates our town down the middle.

With a sigh, I try several more searches to include: "Witches Curse Florence OR", "Wolves and Witches Florence OR", and "Curses from Witches". The last search brings up tons of interesting information regarding curses. Selecting the first article, I settle in to read.

I spend hours poring over the history about different curses cast by witches over the decades. At least the ones that have been chronicled in articles on the witching web. When I finish reading through the last article my search found, I'm impressed by the creativity of my kind, but not any closer to answers on how to save my town.

Sylvia made the witching web sound like it contained information or access to anything that you could possibly need to search for as a witch, but that's obviously not true. Not for the first time, I wonder why the rest of the witches in the town don't seem more concerned about the curse and how it affects our fellow Florence citizens.

Disappointed by my lack of results, I shoot off a text to Sylvia: **wwww is not as helpful as you pretended it was.**

Her reply comes back pretty quickly, considering she's supposed to be cutting mannequin hair: **Even**

Foogle doesn't have all the answers. No website is perfect.

With narrowed eyes, I reply: **Show me the mannequin hair. Or was that just an excuse?**

The picture that comes back has me widening my eyes in horror. What was supposed to be a nice, layered bob is hideously uneven with patchy layers covering the back of the fake head. With a grimace, I type a semi-encouraging, but honest response: **How did you even do that?! Keep practicing, it'll get better!**

Sylvia sends back the cursing emoji, which makes me bust out into laughter. She is great at dyeing hair, especially her own, but maybe not-so-great at haircuts. Hopefully she can improve with practice or just specialize in dye or something.

Placing my phone back down on the bed, I stare at the black and blue screen before me. Without much thought, I pull up MeTube and type in 'Leif Golden'. His page pops up, displaying all his information, including a tiny profile photo. I scroll down and find he's uploaded almost two-hundred videos!

Starting at the very bottom of his MeTube page, I click on his very first video. The date shows it was added over four years ago.

A slightly younger Leif pops up on my screen. His dress and manner are more casual than the video I watched with Sylvia earlier. His hair is shorter and gel-less, and he's wearing a pale blue polo shirt with jeans.

Unlike the confident twenty-something year old I met, this version of Leif seems a bit timid. He barely looks at the camera and talks much softer. In order to hear, I turn the volume on my computer up completely. I listen to Leif as he explains the steps for the potion in his lightly accented timbre. I find this version of Leif much more endearing and can see why people would enjoy watching this shy-seeming guy do magic.

Towards the end of the video, he completes the potion and does his "reveal". Leif dips the ladle into the cauldron and pours the contents into a small, glass jar. He sets the jar on the table, revealing a pale pink liquid that appears so innocent and pretty. The next ladle scoop is poured directly into a vase, and immediately turns into a lush, beautiful bouquet of pale pink roses.

A small smile forms on my face. I'm charmed by this version of Leif, the younger one who posts videos of himself brewing flower potions on the witching web.

Instead of clicking the next video, I pull up a second browser and Foogle search 'Leif Golden' on the witching web. A ton of articles and gossip sites come up with his name. I click through a few, which basically confirm what Sylvia told me about him earlier. Leif's the son of a world-renowned potions master, and a pretty "Hot Bachelor" if the gossip sites are to be believed.

There are a few pictures of him at various events in suave suits, with different dates. The more I learn about Leif, the more of an enigma he seems to become. I wonder if his dad ordered him specifically to come here, and why. In an article I find his dad's name mentioned: Archibald Golden.

Typing Leif's father's name into Foogle populates seven times the number of articles that Leif's name did. Archibald is a part of the Superior Witches' Coven, which apparently oversees all the other Covens. Almost like a Supreme Court for witches. He also runs the Canadian Coven and is believed to have cast a spell in the late 1980's, even though witches' powers were restricted to potions magic at that point.

Pictures show Archibald as a distinguished man, with light brown hair and piercing blue eyes. I click to a picture of Leif, trying to recall if his eyes were that vibrant. Leif's eyes and hair must take after his mother, as the picture shows his eyes are a muddy brown instead of his father's vivid aqua.

I continue my search, curious to find out more about Mrs. Golden. After skimming over a dozen articles, I find a mention of Archibald's daughter, with no name listed, but not a single mention of Mrs. Golden. It's as if she doesn't exist, or at least not according to information available on the witching web.

I spend over an hour reading about the Golden's and by the time I finish, I feel like I know all the information available on the witching web about Leif and his family. With my curiosity semi-satisfied, I return to my browser with Leif's MeTube site and resume watching videos of his potion brewing magic.

Eventually, I flip over to my belly and place the computer on the bed in front of me. My eyelids grow heavy as I continue to click 'Next Video', watching clip after clip of Leif transforming plants into magical potions.

My head gradually drifts downward to rest on my folded arms as I'm halfway through the videos on his feed. At some point, I fall asleep. The last thing I remember is Leif's lightly accented words floating into my ears as he explains the necessary ingredients to brew a transfiguration potion.

4

THE DAILY

Mirabella

Pulling into the parking lot of the Daily the next morning, my eyes instantly scan the parking lot, checking for Vlad's car. It's nowhere in sight, causing me to release a deep sigh of disappointment.

After the quick check, I flip down my visor, using the mirror to delicately extract the blonde strands that have attached themselves to my sticky pink lip gloss. Driving with the windows down always seems like a better idea than the reality. Instead of waking me up more, like I had hoped, it just wreaked havoc on my hair and gloss coated lips.

Once I've successfully removed the gooey strands, I snatch up my purse and march towards the front doors. This is my second Monday at the Daily without Vlad. It feels like everything is measured in the days and hours since he disappeared. The longer he's gone, the more my worry and concern grow. The small rock in my stomach has become a large anvil, dragging me down further with each hour that passes.

Straightening my spine and pushing my shoulders back, I plaster a smile on my face and push through the doors to the lobby. I greet the receptionist, then continue onto my desk, my eyes sliding to Vlad's empty spot across the room—out of habit.

Glenna must catch my quick look, as she stops by my desk while dragging her chair to the front for the morning meeting. "Trouble in Paradise, honey?" Her face looks sincere and concerned.

"Oh, not really." I reply with a shrug. "I think Vlad is just... going through some things."

"Young wolves always are, honey. They always are."

Following her somber words, she continues toward the front, leaving me with my mouth hanging open over her casual mention of the shifters.

I contemplate pumping her for information, in case she knows anything important related to Vlad, then I remember what my grandma said about the town. Almost everyone in Florence is a supernatural of some sort because they spell the town to keep humans away. Apparently, this group of supernatural beings includes Glenna, or at the very least someone Glenna is close with.

Shaking my head, I twirl around to grab my chair and drag it towards the whiteboard. I'm one of the last people to the front. Not wanting to delay the meeting, I quickly settle in with my pad of paper and a pen and turn my attention to Marc.

His gaze sweeps over the group gathered, quickly flitting over me before moving over the rest of his employees in attendance. Things have been odd this week. Marc seems even more tense around me now that Vlad is gone, versus when he was still here and flaunting our newly formed relationship.

Marc turns back towards the whiteboard and claps twice before grabbing a marker. "Okay, who's first? What do you have for me today?"

Hands raise amongst the chairs and ideas are thrown into the meeting. Glenna suggests, "A follow-up on the wolf expo!"

Marc nods slowly, his blocky script adding her idea to the board before pointing at someone else. "Comparison of best sprinkler systems for summer lawn care?" She suggests tentatively.

I observe and listen as the whiteboard slowly fills with ideas. When it's practically full, Marc calls out for final suggestions. I inhale a deep breath to bolster my confidence. For the first time during a morning meeting, I raise my hand into the air.

"Mira," Marc says, an eyebrow quirking up in question or maybe in surprise, as I rarely contribute.

"I think we should do a story on the missing wolves. The town deserves to know what's going on," I state calmly, with my clammy hands clasped in my lap. My words cause one or two small gasps. But as I shift my eyes from Marc to look at my coworkers, I mostly see looks of confusion.

"Like wolves from the woods?" A woman sitting a few seats away asks after a pause, a quizzical look on her face.

My brow scrunches, confused at her response. Has no one else in town noticed shifters are missing? I open my mouth to reply, but Marc claps his hands, effectively cutting me off.

"Okay, thanks for the suggestion, Mira. It doesn't seem like a good idea for this paper, but maybe next time. Let's get started with the ideas we have here," Marc proposes as he scribbles names next to the list on the board. The very last idea he puts his name, then mine, right next to his. "You can work with me today, Mira. We'll get started right away, if you want to come with me to my office."

A pang of panic hits me. His reaction to my story idea makes me feel like I messed up. With dread pooling heavily in my belly, I replace my chair at my desk then trudge into Marc's office.

Without looking up from his computer, he instructs, "If you could please close the door, Mira."

I softly shut the door to the office and think, this is it. This is the day I get fired. An acidic feeling bubbles up my throat, but I swallow it down noisily. Then I take a few deep breaths before returning to face him.

Unless Marc actually fires me, I'm going to ignore his slightly odd behavior. Instead of panicking, I strive for professionalism. "Where should we get started?" I ask politely, sitting in a chair across from his desk.

Marc finally looks up from his computer with a sigh. Steepling his hands in front of him on the desk, he stares at the wall behind me and appears to struggle with his thoughts. A few unreadable expressions flit across his face before his eyes meet mine. "I want you to tell me the truth, Mira. How do you know about the wolves?"

The dread that I had tamed to lie dormant rears its head once more, causing my hands to become clammy and my mouth to dry. I stammer out a response with wide eyes, surprised by his serious nature, "I found an injured wolf the other day... something." I pause, searching for the words to explain what I saw. "Something happened and triggered his shift. I was with Vlad, and the wolf just shifted into a guy. Into Eric."

His eyes harden, "A shifter named Eric just changed into a human right in front of you?"

"Yes," I reply cautiously, wondering why I feel like I'm being interrogated by my typically friendly boss. "He was injured and wasn't in the right... head space. When he turned back into a human, he was in rough shape. Eventually he ended up at the Community Hall."

"You aren't covering for Vlad, are you?" His tone is accusatory and his emerald eyes scream with unspoken suspicion.

Feeling like I've been called in the principal's office and wrongfully accused of a serious offense, like bringing a weapon to school, I try to defend myself and Vlad. "No, not at all. I was at Vlad's house and we heard a strange noise coming from the woods. He told me to stay inside while he checked out the backyard, but I followed him out. Right at the edge of the woods behind his house there was an injured wolf, laying on the ground in a puddle of blood. I moved closer to check and see if it was going to live, or if there was anything we could do to help."

I pause in my story, vividly remembering how Eric looked before he shifted back. "The wolf was in terrible shape and didn't look like it was going to make it. I said a few soft words and tried to pet him, hoping to offer some comfort before he passed. Then he transformed into a human. I don't even know what happened after that. I fainted."

As I tell my story, the tension seems to drain away from Marc's body. His gaze softens and instead of appearing angry, he's contemplative. He doesn't respond, but keeps his emerald gaze locked on mine after I finish speaking.

"What's going on, Marc?" I ask after an unbearable moment of silence.

Marc inhales a deep breath, then flattens his hands against the desk. "How much do you know of the history between the wolves and witches, Mira?" He asks in lieu of responding.

"Not much," I reply hesitantly, unsure of where this conversation is heading.

My grandmother told the story about how a curse

on the town affected witches' magic, but she never mentioned the shifters. I don't think she knew about their curse. Vlad gave me the outline of the shifter curse, but didn't mention a history with the witches. So far, I have knowledge of dual curses with no real connection between the two.

He nods, like I answered the way he expected. Marc pushes his chair away from his desk and stands, then sits back down again. His odd behavior isn't helping calm my nerves at all.

"Okay," he finally says. He pauses briefly with his eyes focused on the wall behind me again. When his emerald colored eyes connect with mine, he continues, "I can tell you what I know. A few hundred years ago, two shifters born of prominent families were engaged to be married. However, three days before the wedding, one of the wolves ran off with another and wed in secret. The wolf that was scorned went to a witch and asked for a curse to be cast. Although this wasn't unheard of, it was uncommon. Wolves and witches knew of one another, but rarely interacted."

"Was this in Florence? What happened next?" I ask, wide-eyed and engrossed in his tale.

Marc looks speculative. "This was a few hundred years ago. I'm not sure if Oregon was even on the map yet. From what I've always heard, this happened in New England."

This gives me pause. From what my grandmother told me; the curse had originated in Florence. I assumed the alleged wedding was between a witch and a shifter which was the reason behind the animosity between the two races. I keep my thoughts to myself though and encourage Marc to continue. "Okay, what did the curse do?"

"Well, it backfired," Marc states simply. "The scorned wolf wanted all wolves to be cursed. The intention of the spell was to create terrible consequences for any wolf that broke their word or promise. She was hoping to prevent any future shifters from having to suffer the embarrassment and heartache that she did." Marc shrugs like that's the end of the story.

"No way, you can't stop there. How did it backfire?" I prod again.

Marc chuckles at my enthusiasm, despite the morbid history we're discussing. "Well, the curse was very complicated and should have never been attempted by one witch alone. For a very complicated spell, multiple strong witches working together helps ensure the potion is the right strength to create the intended outcome. But this witch was renowned for her skill in many categories: reading the future, spell casting, potions, just to name a few. She believed she was strong enough to do it on her own."

"So, this witch was arrogant and her arrogance cursed everyone."

"Basically," Marc replies with a shrug. "Instead of cursing the wolves to keep their promises to others, it made them obligated to keep their word to their wolf, essentially. The witch's curse created a punishment for any shifter that ignored their baser urges—the ones that cause the shift—if ignored, the shifter would turn into their wolf and remain that way permanently."

"Are all shifters cursed then? How did witches become cursed?" I ask, enthralled with Marc's story.

Marc nods again. "Curses can be complex and carry dire consequences if they're not cast correctly. The curse the witch cast... Well, obviously something went wrong. It cursed all the shifters, but the cost was high."

My brow furrows, and Marc backtracks to offer an explanation. "There is always a cost that comes with a curse. You must sacrifice something in order for a curse to stick. The witch who cast the curse didn't plan appropriately, and her mistake caused witches to be stripped of all of their magical powers except potion brewing, to pay the toll of the curse."

The room is absolutely silent. Even the office outside seems unusually still and quiet. Shifting to the edge of the seat, I lean forward, eager to hear more. This is the most information anyone has given me, and I hope Marc hasn't finished explaining yet.

"The curse wasn't well-known, and even the most experienced of witches have been unable to break it. There's also the fear that if the wrong spell is attempted, it may make things worse instead of better," Marc finishes.

My eyes are the size of saucers. "How do you know all this?" I ask quietly.

Marc sighs. "It's complicated, but my family has always been into documenting history. They have an expansive archive on witching history back in Connecticut."

"Is that why you're so into writing the news?" I inquire curiously.

A smile blooms on Marc's face. "Something like that."

The plot was a bit lost for a minute, but suddenly I remember how this conversation started. "Okay, but what does all this have to do with me knowing about shifters?"

Marc's face sobers immediately. "Shifters tried to get the witches to reverse the curse, but like I said before, no one knew the exact spell. Since the magic became so mutilated, no one has found the cure. After the curse, shifters slowly isolated themselves from the witches, to avoid future magic that would further threaten their existence. Over time, witches have slowly forgotten that shifters exist, like the shifters intended. To continue keeping their existence hidden, the shifter council passed a law against revealing your wolf's form to a witch. The offense is punishable by death."

"Unbelievable," I say. The word is not enough to express how I feel, but it's all that I can think of. "I can see why you were so concerned," I tell Marc.

"I hoped that wasn't why Vlad has been MIA as of late," he confesses. "His parents called me last week to explain he needed to go out of town to attend family business... But I've seen you moping around and eyeing his desk. The whole situation just seemed," he thinks before continuing. "It just all seemed off."

"Well," I begin, "Things are a bit strange right now," I admit to Marc. "Vlad isn't in trouble with the Council, at least not really... or maybe not yet. We were in the woods the other day and some other wolves appeared. They were acting strange. And then suddenly Vlad leapt into the air, shifted into a giant wolf, and ran away with the others," I whisper with a hard edge to my tone. "I'm not really sure what's going on with him right now."

Marc nods slowly. "Well, I know your families are close and he's important to you. I'm glad you're alright and I'm sure he will be too." He claps his hands together after his words of encouragement. "Okay, how about we stop talking about things we can't change and work on this story instead?"

"Can I ask one more question before we move on?"

"Sure," Marc replies, giving me his undivided attention.

I had forgotten how warm it felt to be on the receiving end of his emerald gaze. He becomes so focused on you, like you're the only person in the world. "Do any of the other witches in town know of the shifters?"

"None of the others are aware of them, at least as far as I know. Like I said, despite living in close quarters, the shifters prefer to keep their existence a secret from anyone that could do them harm. And that certainly includes witches." After a few seconds of silence, Marc asks, "Anything else?"

I decline with a shake of my head and Marc grins, his beautiful teeth glinting as they're exposed to the light. "Let's dig into our story then."

"Sounds good to me. What are we working on again? Sorry, I kind of spaced out when you were handing out the assignments."

"Let me double check," Marc says, pulling over his notepad where he jotted down the assignments from the board. "It looks like we're working on a story about safe methods for gopher extermination." He looks up from his notepad and the second his eyes connect with mine, we both burst into laughter.

"I guess we better get started. Gopher lives are at stake," I joke once I get my giggles under control.

Marc nods and shifts his computer screen to the side, providing us both with a view of the screen. "Let's save the gophers."

I SHUT the door to Marc's office gently behind me, returning to my desk after hours upon hours of gopher research. I'm feeling accomplished after completing the simple task of drafting our article. Plus, a little lighter after sharing a good amount of laughter with Marc.

He makes everything feel more... normal.

The second I reach my desk, some of my pep fades as my eyes catch on Vlad's desk. I replay my conversation with Marc as I eye the empty chair. The curse is so much larger than what I thought. It's affecting witches and shifters everywhere, yet no one appears to be searching for answers. Hopelessness threatens to creep in as I mull over my earlier conversation, but I vehemently shut it out. Forcing a deep inhale, I open my desk drawer to reveal my purse. As I gather my belongings, I attempt to stop thinking of Vlad and the idea that he could be in trouble.

It isn't until I take a couple of steps towards the exit, ready to leave for the day, that I realize something I didn't ask Marc... nor did he volunteer the information himself. Besides his family's interest in history, he never told me about his own affiliation with the curse.

At this point, I'm not even sure if Marc is a witch or a shifter.

5

THE BULLY

Mirabella

The minute my feet hit the paved parking lot outside the Daily, a text message from an unknown number pops up onto my screen with a ding. I click on the message, hoping it's from Vlad. **Hey, this is Leif. Your gma gave me your number. Are we still on for this afternoon?**

When I see who it is, or I guess who it isn't, I'm not as disappointed as I expected to be. With a small smile, I type back a quick message: **Hey Leif, I'm just leaving work. I'll be over soon and we'll go for our ice cream!**

I shove my phone into my purse and dig out the keys to my Prius. Now that I've thought of ice cream, I realize how hot it is outside. Rain is the norm in Oregon, but occasionally we get a small heat wave during the summer. This year, the weather has fluctuated dramatically, but today is sweltering hot.

Sliding into my seat, I start my car and immediately jab the buttons to get my air conditioner blasting. With the cool air started, I buckle up and check my mirrors before pulling onto the road and heading to my grandmother's house.

I try to arrange the information disclosed by Marc into bite-sized tidbits that will be easy for my grandma, and maybe Leif, to digest, while I drive. I'm hopeful they'll be able to offer me suggestions on how to proceed. We need to find more information about the curse, the cure, and how to save the shifters and help the witches.

I'm so lost in thought, the distance passes in what feels like seconds. Once my grandmother's tree cottage is visible, my mind snaps back to the present. I turn off my car and hop out to jog up the small set of stairs.

Normally my grandmother is waiting on the steps when I arrive, and I'm surprised to see she isn't outside today. I move forward and firmly knock on her red door twice, hoping I'll be able to discuss what I've learned.

A minute goes by and I'm about to knock again when the door creaks open to reveal Leif. Well, Leif's chest covered in a light blue t-shirt. Standing this close to him, I have to crane my neck back to meet his gaze.

When my eyes finally reach his face, he has an intense look that I'm not sure how to interpret. I choose to ignore it and ask, "Hey Leif, is my grandma home? I wanted to run a few things by her really quick before we head into town."

Leif declines with a shake of his head. "She left an hour or two ago. Said she had a top priority bunko game at her friend Marjorie's."

I've never heard of this friend before, but that doesn't mean much. My grandma is a social butterfly and seems to know everyone and everything that's happening around town, despite living in a tree in the woods.

Tamping down my disappointment over her absence, I ask Leif, "Well, are you ready to hit the town then?" A huge grin appears on his face. His excitement makes him look like a young child. It's contagious, and a smile slides onto my face in response.

"I'm almost ready." He gestures to his feet. "I just need to grab my shoes. Did you want to come inside?" He asks, stepping back to provide room for me to enter.

Nodding, I step inside the cottage and wander to stand near one of the bookshelves. Leif hustles by me, gently squeezing my shoulder as he passes, heading further into the home. As he disappears from sight, I realize I've never seen the back portion of my grandma's house.

I war with my curiosity, taking a step inside the kitchen and towards the back hallway. My eyes skim down a row of closed doors as my mind plays with the idea of opening a few of them.

Leif reappears from the second to last door as I take my first step into the hall. He quirks a brow and asks, "Ready?"

We drive the few minutes downtown in silence. When we reach the first intersection, I glance at Leif and find him staring out the window at Florence, not paying any attention to me. I return my gaze to the road and continue driving.

We're forced to wind through the streets twice before I'm able to find a parking spot. The Parlor is teeming with activity, the line spilling out onto the sidewalk and wrapping around the side of the building. Apparently, ice cream was everyone's first thought when the heat wave struck.

"This is Downtown Florence?" Leif asks, looking around as he exits the car.

I follow his gaze and imagine what it would be like to be an outsider, seeing Florence for the first time. Majority of the buildings are squat, brick structures with vibrant signage to differentiate each shop from its neighbor. A few painted buildings are interspersed, but most of downtown looks the same. As I glance around, I wonder what Leif's hometown looks like. Are there skyscrapers or is it a sleepy little town like ours?

Muddy eyes connect with mine, and I remember Leif asked a question. "Yes, this is it. Welcome to Florence." I finally say, throwing my arms out to encompass the area surrounding us.

Leif tilts his chin at me. "I like it. It feels very... quaint."

That's a yes to skyscrapers then, I think to myself with a smile. "Let's head over to get our ice cream."

Together we walk along the sidewalk, the heat

causing a trickle of sweat to drip down my back. I glance at Leif under my lashes, inspecting him as he walks. He doesn't seem affected by the heat, despite wearing jeans. Either he is more composed than I am, or he's used to hotter summers than this.

We make it to the Parlor and queue up at the end of the line. Luckily, we are just close enough to be covered by the shade provided by the forest green awning, a small respite from the heat.

I quietly watch the family in front of us struggle to wrangle their kids into decorum, while the line slowly shuffles forward. To the parent's relief and the kids delight, the wait is short and all of us are in the shop within a few moments.

A teenage boy steps up to help the family and I laugh as the kids scream and point at the glass, requesting their desired flavors. A teenage girl approaches the counter near Leif and I, stealing my attention away from the family.

"How can I help you?" she asks, with a slight stammer.

I look to Leif, and he gestures for me to go ahead. "Uhm, do you still have Cherry Garcia?" I ask. She wordlessly points to the tub of pink colored ice cream, dotted with red chunks, positioned in front of us.

"Right, well, I'll take a scoop of that in a cone," I order, my cheeks only slightly heated from embarrassment. I step towards the register while Leif orders, but when I make a move to pay, his hand shoots in front of mine with a twenty-dollar bill in his grasp.

"This is for both of us," he tells the kid behind the register.

"Oh, you don't have to do that. I can pay for mine," I respond, my five-dollar bill still clasped in my hand.

"I know I don't 'have to', but it's my pleasure. Thank you for showing me what Florence has to offer," Leif says with a wink.

"Well, thank you," I reply, my cheeks blushing furiously over his rapt attention.

Leif collects his change from the cashier, and we head outside. He makes a beeline to one of the bistro tables on the sidewalk. I trail behind, my eyes focused on my ice cream cone, licking off the small drops that are melting down the sides.

Before I can make it to the table, a whirlwind of silky, chestnut hair appears before me. Next thing I know, my ice cream cone connects with my face, splattering across my nose as a palm shoves against my shoulder, pushing me to the ground. I'm barely able to throw my hands behind me in time to catch myself.

On my butt with my legs sprawled in front of me, my scraped hands behind me, and ice cream covering my face and shirt, I look up to see the perpetrator. Kaylee's face hovers above me wearing a malicious expression. "Guess you better watch where you're going, little Mir," She taunts.

A wave of laughter follows her words, but it barely registers. My blood is boiling at her usage of Vlad's nickname, but I don't reply and stay seated on the ground. I know she'll quickly tire of taunting me if I don't fight back. I just need to sit and wait her out. Then once she leaves, I can scrape my dignity, and myself, off the ground.

"Where's Vlad?" Kaylee taunts, "Did he get tired of slumming it already? We all knew that wouldn't last. The Quarterback and the loser."

Laughter from the side continues to punctuate her comments. I don't bother to turn my head. I already know who her groupies are and am not worried about confirming my tormentors. I space out, waiting for Kaylee to leave, when a flash of blonde hair catches my attention from the corner of my eye.

Leif strides into view and stands directly in front of me, offering a hand to help me off the ground. Without meeting his eyes, I gingerly lift a slightly injured palm from the sidewalk and place it into his. He tugs me to my feet with ease, then surprises me when he wraps his arm around my shoulder and pulls my ice cream drenched body into his side. He turns us to face Kaylee as a unit.

Leif's pleasant tone surprises me when he asks Kaylee, "And you are?"

Kaylee simpers under anyone's attention, apparently this includes a guy holding a girl she just shoved to the ground. Either that or she recognizes Leif, despite the lack of introduction, and wants to woo him to her friend group.

"Kaylee Williams," she says, fluttering her lashes.

"Well, Miss Kaylee Williams," Leif continues in a polite tone, "I think you owe my friend, Mira Love, an apology." I feel him glance down at me, but I continue to look forward with a dead stare. "It appears you accidentally ruined her ice cream, her top, and... her palms."

Kaylee guffaws instead of responding.

Leif's lack of reaction to her laughter arouses suspicion. My eyes dart to his face and I find a completely neutral expression. I wonder if his antics are going to make things worse with Kaylee in the future.

The second after the thought crosses my mind, a flash of movement from Leif's opposite side catches my eye. The initial throw is fast, like an MLB pitcher fast, but everything afterwards occurs in slow motion.

I watch as an almost translucent liquid spouts from Leif's hand in Kaylee's direction. It hits her mid throat, splashing outwards to douse her shirt and a portion of her face, with a few droplets flying off to soak into the heated pavement.

Her laugh abruptly turns into a splutter, and her hands immediately rise to grab her throat. At first, I think she's just surprised. Her hands raising up to confirm she has, in fact, been targeted by someone else when she's used to being the bully. My smugness quickly turns to horror as she begins to gag and choke. Her hands are frantically clutching her throat, scraping to try to allow air to reach her lungs.

I shove away from Leif with a look of horror. "Leif, what did you do?" I ask quietly, as Kaylee sinks to her knees on the pavement, still gagging and scratching.

"Just teaching her a little lesson, that's all." Leif says

casually, as he watches Kaylee struggle, her lips beginning to turn blue from lack of oxygen.

"Stop it," I demand.

Leif doesn't move, his entire body still with his gaze focused down on Kaylee.

"Right now, Leif. I mean it." I demand again, louder.

He releases a deep sigh and shoots me a look of exasperation. With his brown eyes locked on mine, I hear the snap of his fingers. Immediately after, Kaylee gulps in a large breath of air. Then another.

I'm unable to tear my eyes away from Leif's, as if he has me hypnotized with his gaze. The sound of Kaylee's voice snaps me from the trance. "That was majorly fucked up. And against the rules of the coven," she says. Her voice comes out as a rasp, but she still manages to sound livid. Minor scrapes on her throat, caused by her nails clawing for her airway, have trickles of blood dripping down onto her top.

Leif sounds unconcerned by her accusations. "I'm not from your coven. Their rules don't apply to me." He inspects his fingernails like he can't even be bothered to look at Kaylee while she stomps away, maintaining a glare in our direction.

I watch as she joins her gaggle of friends, who all seem frozen in place from shock. When no one moves she tugs on Greg's arm, forcing him to wrap it around her waist, and then drags him off. She shoots one last glare over her shoulder and the rest of the crew slowly follows behind them, studiously avoiding looking in our direction.

Ignoring their departure entirely, Leif turns towards me. "Are you okay, Mira Love?" His tone is surprisingly gentle, considering he almost just murdered someone for shoving an ice cream cone in my face.

"I'm... fine," I respond hesitantly. "I think I just want to go home; I need to clean up." I gesture to my face and shirt, which are coated with sticky, pink ice cream.

Leif nods. His gaze searches mine, and I barely contain a flinch as a flash of Kaylee's struggle jumps to the front of my mind. "I can drive. You seem a bit shaken up."

A bit shaken up seems like kind of an understatement.

6

THE CANADIAN

Mirabella

I emerge from my bathroom lost in thought and toweling off my hair. It's taking all of my focus to avoid replaying the scene with Kaylee at the parlor, over and over. I'm doing anything I can to keep my mind otherwise occupied.

My phone rings from my bedside table and I approach it warily, hoping the call isn't from Leif. Thankfully, it's Sylvia's name flashing across the screen. I accept the call and place the phone next to my ear, "Hey."

"Oh, my gosh. Your texts were insane! I read them on my lunch break and then almost ditched half my day at school to come see you. Are you okay?" Sylvia asks. Her words fly at me in a steady barrage, tinged with concern.

"I'm..." I take a deep breath to buy time while I collect my thoughts. I'm not sure how I am yet.

I've been avoiding thoughts of Leif's over-the-top actions this afternoon and our uncomfortable car ride back to my house. I've even avoided thoughts of Leif meeting my mom, then telling me he'd find his own way back to my grandma's house, despite the innocence of those actions. I've pushed it all away while I focused on showering.

"I'm not really sure," I finally answer.

Sylvia hmms in response.

"I feel like it was insane. As much as I've wished someone would put Kaylee in her place for years, I still felt bad for her. If I hadn't said anything..." I pause, unsure if I should voice the thought that's been running through my brain, even to Sylvia. Bolstering my courage, I continue, "I think if I hadn't demanded that he stop, Leif would have let her die."

Sylvia gasps. "You don't think that's a bit dramatic? He was probably just trying to scare her."

I can tell Sylvia's skeptical. But, it's different reading the novel-length texts I spammed her with this afternoon versus experiencing the situation firsthand.

"You weren't there, Sylvia. She was scraping at her throat, kneeling on the ground with blue lips. Her posse was too afraid to even move." I shudder, recalling the scene. "Then when she could talk again, she said that was against the coven rules or something, but Leif didn't care."

Sylvia hmms again. "Well yeah, our coven rules

dictate that we're not allowed to use our magic to harm another witch unless it's in self-defense. Considering Leif isn't from our coven... and who his father is, who he is even, I'm not surprised her veiled threat didn't bother him."

We let the silence linger on the line as we think.

"Are you going to see him again?" She asks.

I mull it over. "I don't think I have much of a choice. He traveled here from Canada to help me. Honestly, he seemed a little upset that I wasn't more grateful about what he did to Kaylee. Like he thought he was defending my honor or something."

"Well, he kind of was. Just be careful, in case he causes more trouble. You don't want to be in the middle of a bunch of angry witches," Sylvia advises. As if I hadn't already thought of that myself.

7

THE POTION

Mirabella

The rest of the week, I keep my head down and my ears to the ground for any news regarding Vlad. Or any news of a huge, dark-furred wolf roaming the woods. The days continue to pass without any information surfacing and I stick to my routine. I go to work, eat dinner with my parents, then head upstairs to paint and listen to music. It's the only thing keeping me grounded.

Friday finally rolls around, but instead of being excited for the weekend, I'm hit with a pang of sadness. Work is the best distraction from thoughts of Vlad. I drive home from the Daily with a heavy heart and sit in my parent's driveway for an unusually long time before heading inside.

At six o'clock on the dot, I hear a knock at the front door. I'm puttering around the entryway waiting for

Jacob to finish making some snacks. Assuming it's Sylvia, I open the door without checking the peephole.

Instead of being greeted by the swath of lime green hair I anticipated, I reveal a broad chest covered in a black t-shirt. Craning my neck back, my eyes connect with a pair of muddy eyes. Ones that I haven't necessarily been avoiding, but also haven't specifically sought after the events of Monday evening.

"Mira Love," Leif says, a smirk forming on his lips as he speaks.

We stand there, looking at each other for a beat, then I simply say, "Leif Golden."

His smirk grows larger, taking over his entire face. "I feel you've been avoiding me this week, while you were to help me learn about Florence. As a prelude to your potions lessons." His tone suggests his chastisement is more of a joke than a serious matter.

While waiting for my response, he leans against the doorjamb casually. Like he's been here a hundred times and we're comfortable old friends.

Meanwhile, I'm feeling awkward and unsettled for reasons I can't explain. Part of me wants to make Leif disappear before Sylvia gets here, to avoid any potential fangirl episodes. The other part of me wishes she would show up sooner, to save me from the awkwardness of having to explain to Leif why I haven't been in contact with him since the incident at the Parlor.

When the silence becomes awkwardly long, with Leif's smirk continuing to grow larger, I finally accept he's not leaving without an explanation and Sylvia isn't right around the corner waiting to save me.

"I've just been... a little busy," I say, knowing it sounds like an excuse but unable to think of any other response. "Work has been pretty tough lately," I tack on to the end.

Raising my gray eyes to his expectantly, I see his smirk has fallen and his expression is now contemplative. His next words are unexpected. "I may need to talk to your boss about giving you a few weeks off to prepare for the exams. I'm sure your grandmother and parents would agree obtaining your witching license is more important than writing newspaper articles. Once we brew our first potion together, I'll be able to better gauge where we stand and how long it should take to prepare you. After you pass, you can go back to your regular work schedule at the Daily."

His tone assumes I'm going to thank him and readily agree to his new plan for my life. Maybe he's used to getting his way, but I'm not going to bend to his will without a fight. "I don't want to give up working at the Daily," I respond firmly.

Leif's eyes jump from the top of the door, to my face. "Mira Love," he starts. His tone sounds like he's speaking with a child, causing my hackles to rise. "I'm here to help you pass your witches exams, as quickly as possible, so you can find answers to help your friends. If that's what you want, you may have to make a few sacrifices to achieve that goal, such as limiting your time at the Daily during your studies."

The Daily is the only thing I have left that's tying me to Vlad.

"What if I cut back to only four days a week?" I propose as a compromise, as I fight the urge to slam the door on Leif and this conversation.

I want to save the town, but I can do that without giving up the Daily. I think.

Leif's face looks skeptical. "Your job made you too busy to spend any time with me this week. We could've been getting to know each other and starting potion brewing. I definitely don't think you have enough time for both. But I'll think about it before I go to your boss on Monday."

I guess the consequences of avoiding Leif are losing my job at the Daily. Bitterness wells up in the back of my throat like bile, but I swallow it down and offer a nod.

"Can I come in? We can start brewing tonight," Leif suggests, straightening from his casual lean.

Before I can respond, I hear a loud huff of air and the sound of sneakers slapping across paved ground coming from behind Leif. Within seconds, a shock of green hair becomes visible at the bottom of the lawn.

Leif turns to the side, following the direction of my gaze and together we watch Sylvia, sprinting towards my front door from the bottom of the driveway. Her face is pink and her chest is heaving, with one small trickle of sweat running down from her forehead, as if she'd run a mile before heading over to my house.

She stops on the front stoop and bends in half,

with her hands resting on her knees as she tries to catch her breath. Leif and I watch as she gulps in huge breaths of air, before straightening into a normal, upright standing position.

"Ran. All. The. Way. Here." She pants between breaths.

I forgo pointing out that she may need more cardio, if she's this out of breath from running down the block. Normally I love to tease Sylvia, but I don't want to embarrass her in front of her celebrity witch crush.

"Leif Golden, and you are...?" Leif states, holding his hand out for Sylvia to shake.

"Sylvia Amica, Mira's best friend," Sylvia says with gusto, like she's proud to be my best friend. Then she shakes Leif's hand heartily.

I smile at her, grateful she interrupted and hopeful she'll be able to scare Leif off.

"As you can see," I begin, pointing to Sylvia. "I already have plans for tonight and can't brew potions with you."

"Oh, are you here to brew potions?" Sylvia interjects, her pale eyes pinging between Leif and I. "I could just tag along. We could do it here. In your parents' witching chamber downstairs."

I try to shoot Sylvia a look—one that says "take that offer back right this second or I'll never forgive you"—but she's looking up at Leif, instead of down in my direction.

"Sounds like a great idea to me. Why don't you ladies lead the way, eh?" Leif responds politely, his accent sounding heavier than usual, in Sylvia's presence.

Stifling my groan, I pivot and head for the stairs, resigned to Leif invading my Friday night plans with Sylvia. Before I climb the first step, Jacob appears in the hallway. "Are you ready for the snacks, Ms. Love?"

Leif smoothly steps forward and offers, "I can take them, sir."

Jacob quirks a brow, then gives a quick nod. He scurries away towards the kitchen without another word. Leif glances at me, then trails behind him silently.

I stay near the bottom step with Sylvia, resting against the railing while we wait for Leif to return. He reappears with an entire tray laden with mostly junk food, and one small plate of veggies with a dip.

Jacob didn't return with Leif, but I still yell, "Thank you, Jacob!"

Afterwards, I climb the steps followed by my friend and the guy who can't seem to take a hint.

If you told me two months ago that I would be in a circular stone cellar with my best friend and a quasi-underground celebrity, learning the correct way to add a "pinch" of something to a pewter cauldron, I would've called a mental institution to pick you up. There is no way I would've believed that was an accurate prediction for one of my future Friday nights. Yet, here we are.

"No, no. That's way too much for a pinch, Mira Love." Leif places his fingers over mine, using them to adjust my grip. The action transmits a light shock. I force myself not to react and listen to his words. "Yes, just like that. Okay, I'm going to step back and you can continue."

Leif's original instructions were to brew a potion while he watched. He said he could gauge my skill level while I worked, then use that information to create a lesson plan for the witches exams. Instead of letting me brew, however, he interjects non-stop to correct me. An hour in and we've only gotten through three steps.

Sylvia has not been helpful to my cause. She's seated in one of the navy armchairs near the fireplace, crunching through snacks and watching Leif and I like we're her favorite soap opera.

Glancing around, I spot a notepad I abandoned last week on the corner of the table. Snatching it up, I offer it to Leif. He accepts it cautiously with a quizzical expression. "What if you just write the corrections you'd like to make and let me brew the potion? Then you can add the errors I make into your lesson plan," I suggest. "You could even sit in the armchair opposite of Sylvia, to observe."

Leif shakes his head. "I'll write everything down that I see, but it will be easier to observe from over here. Go ahead and brew the potion."

I nod, then attempt to ignore Leif and focus on my potion. Rolling back my shoulders, I pull the instructions closer.

One drop of Iliad liquid. Done.

One leaf of aspen. Added.

One pinch of prism powder. Check.

Only two more steps remain, then stirring. Hopefully all the rest will go smoothly.

Reading the next line, I pull over the jar filled with Mandora roots, snap one in half and add it to the mixture in the cauldron. Lastly, I take the glowing rima liquid and shake in two drops from the container.

Glancing at Leif, I pick up the ladle to stir. He gives me an encouraging nod, and I proceed to stir. Six times clockwise and seven times counterclockwise, just like the directions say. Once the liquid stops swirling in the cauldron, I grab the clear vial sitting nearby and add a ladle of my potion.

I step away from the table to an empty portion of the stone floor, then throw the vial down. The glass shatters and the liquid puddles on the ground. You could hear a pin drop as the three of us watch expectantly, like the smoke screen it's supposed to make is running late or something.

After a full minute of nothingness, I release a sigh and throw myself into the armchair across from Sylvia. Placing my arm over my eyes, I groan out, "I'm the world's worst witch."

A set of large fingers place a firm, but gentle grip over my wrist and tug my arm upwards with another shock. I glance up, expecting Leif to be hovering over me. To my surprise, he's on his haunches in front of the chair, making himself eye level with my much shorter and seated frame.

"Mira," He starts in a soft tone, one that feels strangely intimate for near-strangers. "No witch has ever started out as 'the best witch'. It's a skill, and like all skills, it requires patience and persistence to hone. Becoming an expert potion brewer, or even a novice brewer, won't happen overnight. That's why I'm here to train you. I've never had a witch I've trained fail their exams, and I will not let you change that statistic." He finishes his pep talk with a smirk, highlighting the slight dig.

"I just don't know what I'm doing wrong, besides pinching too much when I go to add a 'pinch'," I cry, exasperated.

Leif rubs his chin with his right hand, and I realize his left still has a grip on my wrist. I wriggle my hand around, but Leif tightens his fingers, instead of releasing me. His gaze meets mine and we stare each other down.

I'm fighting the urge to blink when a sudden crunch breaks the tense atmosphere. Startled, I look over Leif's shoulder and see Sylvia watching us with wide eyes, while shoveling chips into her mouth.

Her lips struggle to contain the snack, with a few crumbs flying free as she mumbles, "Didn't mean to interrupt. Please continue the weird staring thing." Except her voice is mutilated from her snacks and her words come out elongated and garbled.

I chuckle at her antics, then turn my attention back

to Leif waiting for an answer. I'm hoping that maybe he saw something simple, something he can easily correct, when he watched me brew my potion. When he doesn't speak, I raise an eyebrow to reinforce my unspoken question.

"Witches can be affected by their environment. It's very common for witches to only brew in one location, become comfortable, then seem unable to brew somewhere new without added effort."

I open my mouth to interject, but Leif silences me with a glare. "I don't think that's the case for you, since you haven't been able to successfully brew a potion, at all."

Now it's my turn to glare at Leif. Obviously if I wasn't a failure at being a witch, he wouldn't be here to teach me how to be better.

Ignoring the look, Leif continues, "I think the issue you're having, is that your emotions are too close to the surface, which is affecting the effectiveness of your potions. You're so fixated on the idea that you can't do this, that you're rendering your own potions ineffective with that thought/feeling."

I open, then close my mouth. Thinking on his words, I try to determine whether they could be true. When I made the green smoke, I guess I was rather nervous. During the process, I thought *what if I accidentally kill someone*? At least a few times.

Leif's next words interrupt the epiphany he inspired, "Do you believe you can do this, Mira?"

"Well, kind of..." I respond, tentatively.

"Kind of is neither yes nor very confidence inspiring," Leif quips back.

His words hit a nerve. "I literally just found out magic is real and now it feels like everyone is counting on me. I'm only a girl. One who's good at art and that's it…"

I pause, inhaling deeply and plunging into the thoughts I've been too fearful to voice. "I can't even save myself from being bullied by a bunch of teenagers. Instead, I spent years hiding in the bathroom and eating lunch in the library. How am I supposed to save anyone else, when I wasn't even able to defend myself?"

As the words spill out of me, I realize how freeing it is to say the truth out loud. I don't think I'm cut out for this. I couldn't save myself. I couldn't help Vlad. I don't want all this pressure. Or to ruin people's lives if I can't succeed… because I'm not confident that I can.

Leif stands, shifting his wrist and issuing another shock. I hiss in annoyance and blurt, "Also, could you please stop shocking me?"

His brow furrows. and he quickly releases me and strides away. From the way he moves, it's clear that he's given up on me too. Part of me is relieved to no longer be under the immense pressure of saving the world. But the other part is disappointed that my magic isn't strong enough to help.

My eyes follow Leif as he wanders to one of the shelves lining the circular walls of the witching chamber. He skims his finger across the spines of the books, suddenly stopping halfway across and pulling a single leather-bound text from the shelf.

He returns to my chair and rests on the arm, opening the book to a random page before looking down at me. "Do you know what this is?" He asks.

I shake my head to indicate I don't.

With a slow nod, Leif shifts the book so I'm able to see the page he's looking at. It appears to be a very old family tree. Pointing to the top, he says, "These are the original witching families. It all started with these five."

My eyes skim across the names and widen.

I receive another slow nod from Leif when I meet his gaze. "Your mom and your grandma are from a legacy family. Descendants from one of the original witching bloodlines. Two full-blooded witches came together to create you, one of whom was a legacy. Do you know what that means?"

I shake my head again, feeling like I know nothing. The same feeling I've had since my world turned upside down on my eighteenth birthday.

"It means, Mira Love, that you are powerful." He pauses, tapping a finger against the book. "Also, I haven't been shocking you, but I've heard of this happening before. Your magic sparks whenever you're around other supernatural beings."

My eyes widen in surprise. "So, I'm like a magic detector?" I ask.

Leif nods, "Something like that. Your magic is innate and strong. You've been using it without even knowing. If any single witch could do this, it would be you. Or maybe me," He jokes with another one of his signature smirks.

I laugh, and in the background, I hear Sylvia chuckle as well.

"Maybe we could do it together." I suggest, feeling more confident. Both the book showing I'm a legacy and Leif placing his faith in me, make me want to do better.

He shrugs in response, flipping the book closed and placing it on my lap.

I hug the tome to my chest and glance around the witching chamber, feeling mildly uncomfortable now that our emotional chat has finished. "What do we do now?"

"Well, Mira Love. Now that we've settled that, I think it's time to brew some more potions."

8

THE WARNING

Mirabella

The next day, I wake up to my alarm blaring. My head feels heavy and my brain groggy, like I got half an hour of sleep. Honestly, that may be an accurate estimate, as I tossed and turned most of the night after Leif and Sylvia went home.

Picking up my phone to turn off my alarm, I notice Marc sent a message over an hour ago, which causes a surge of panic to course through me. I check the time on my phone, then double check with the alarm clock I bought when I was constantly late to work. I breathe a sigh of relief when I confirm I'm not late. Then I laugh at myself when the little calendar on the upper corner of my phone catches my eye.

Today's Saturday. I must've set my alarm out of habit.

My curiosity piqued by Marc's message on a Saturday, I click the icon on my phone to open the text. My good humor instantly turns to anger. I forgot about the brief conversation Leif, and I had yesterday, concerning my job at the Daily. Apparently, it was much more serious and meaningful to him than it was to me.

Marc's message reads: **Had a VERY early conversation this morning with your new potion trainer. Wish you would have told me the Daily was interfering with your practice. Leif and I came to an agreement for a lighter workload. Your new schedule is 7am-11am M-W. See you Monday.**

Although nothing in the message directly states he's upset, I can tell Marc isn't happy that Leif contacted him in my place. I can't say that I'm thrilled about it either.

I type out a quick response, hoping to smooth things over: **Sorry, Marc. Leif was very persistent that I lighten my workload, but he told me we could talk about it some more before I asked for fewer hours. Thank you for being understanding. See you Monday.**

Clicking to my messages with Leif, I type up a text to express my frustration. After I finish typing, I read over my words and realize it all sounds very childish. I delete the message and start over. I do this at least ten times. Type, read, delete, and repeat.

Eventually, I give up and place my phone on the nightstand with a sigh. It's annoying that Leif went over my head this morning, instead of waiting until

Monday like we discussed. I know I need to concentrate on building my potion brewing skills, but I also don't want to lose the Daily, or my connection with Vlad. Despite my irritation, I don't think Leif was acting maliciously and it wouldn't be fair to lash out.

I flip over and fluff up my pillow before laying back down. Closing my eyes, I try to chase after sleep, since I don't need to be awake before dawn on Saturday. Instead of sleeping, my mind replays my victory from last night.

After the talk with Leif about being a legacy, we disposed of the dud potion and started brewing the same recipe again, together. Within twenty minutes we had a bubbling cauldron of clear liquid. I bottled a ladle full, threw it on the ground and had a smoke screen like they use in fake magic shows.

Thinking of my success causes me to grin ear to ear and any lingering anger at Leif dissipates. His method was underhanded, but honestly his advice so far has been accurate. Maybe giving up some time at the Daily is the right next step. And it's not forever, just until I'm able to get my witching license.

The thought has my blood thrumming through my veins in excitement, and I immediately give up any hope I had about falling back asleep. I fling my covers to the side and wander to my closet. There I take my time donning a pair of paint splattered jeans and a comfortable pale blue top, then I tie my hair back in a ribbon. After a quick check in the mirror for crusted drool or anything else gross or embarrassing, I leave my room.

The second my feet hit the wooden floor of the foyer, a knock sounds at the front door. Startled, I walk over and check the peephole. My eye sweeps across the visible areas of the porch, but I can't see anyone standing there.

Cautiously, I open the door and a piece of paper flutters to the ground, like someone placed it in the crevice between the door and the frame. I pick up the sheet of paper, then take a step forward. Looking left, then right, I try to find the person who knocked and/or left the note, but there isn't a soul in sight.

Our street still appears sleepy, bathed in the dusky morning sun. Porch lights are still on, cars in driveways, and a resounding silence from the neighborhood, all confirm that no one is out and about yet. It's Saturday, after all.

With one last sweeping look, I step back inside and firmly shut the front door. I remember the paper, which is now crumpled from being clutched in my grasp. Leaning against the closed door, I smooth the wrinkles, then turn it upright. Before I'm able to read the words on the page, a glimpse of Jacob's gray hair catches my eye.

He calls out, "Good morning, Ms. Love." But he does not stop his quick clip as he walks through the hallway connecting the kitchen and the sitting room.

"Oh, Jacob! Wait," I reply, my words halting him in

his tracks. "Did you see anyone around the house earlier? Or hear a knock?"

"No, Ms. Love," Jacob replies, a small frown crossing his weathered face. "Is something amiss?"

"No, no," I reassure him. "Someone just left a note in the door." I gesture to the paper in my hand. "It's probably a flier or something, I'll just throw it away." I straighten from the door, under the pretense of walking to the kitchen to place the paper in the garbage.

Jacob offers a brief dip of his head before continuing to the sitting room.

I meander towards the kitchen until he's out of sight, then stop in the hallway. I change directions to run back upstairs and make a beeline to my room. With the door firmly closed, I straighten out the note.

It's a plain white piece of paper, like it came from someone's printer. Scrawled across the page are seven words written in black paint. The letters are all capitalized and boldly written, with the paint dripping slightly down the page, as if it were barely given the chance to dry.

I read the message, a chill sweeping down my spine.

LEIF CANNOT BE TRUSTED. WATCH YOUR BACK.

Then, I read it three more times before carefully folding the page into quarters. I open the bottom drawer to my nightstand and pull out a sketchbook, then carefully place the note inside to show Sylvia later today.

Straightening, I shake out my arms, trying to relieve some tension that's built in my body over the last few minutes. With an outward calm, I walk back down the stairs, intent on making something to eat. I enter the kitchen with the painted words playing on repeat in my head. Their meaning, both vague and clear, echoes through my thoughts for the rest of the morning.

9

THE TOAD

Mirabella

I triple check my ingredients on the table, mentally checking off each one with my manual. After I confirm I've gathered the accurate leaves, liquids, powders, and roots, I drop each item into the cauldron, one-by-one. Within minutes, I have a pale-yellow bubbling liquid, as expected.

A grin takes over my face and I bottle two vials of the liquid, before turning off the burner underneath my cauldron. With a deep breath and a small prayer, I throw one to the ground. On impact, the glass shatters and the pale-yellow liquid covers the floor. Holding my breath, I watch as it quickly morphs into a large, green toad.

Shrieking, I throw my arms in the air and jump up and down. "I did it! I did it!"

The door to the witching chamber slams open,

startling me mid shriek and cutting my celebration short. My dad bursts forward, a mask on his face, wielding a broom like a weapon. His eyes scan the room searching for a threat before landing on the toad. He slowly lowers the broom and pulls off his mask, revealing a delighted expression.

Over my dad's shoulder, I glimpse my mom's blonde hair as she peeks into the room. "What did she create this time?" She asks in a tentative voice, her words carried across the room by the circular stones.

"A toad!" My dad exclaims, turning to look at my mom. His gray eyes flash with elation. "It's a toad!"

My mom releases an excited gasp, then steps fully into view. A pair of large gardening shears are clutched in her hands as she rushes forward, towards me. I back up as she approaches, fearing I'll end up accidentally stabbed by the sharp, bladed ends. My mom's brow furrows, until I give a pointed look at the shears, she's still holding in a death grip.

"Oh," my mom says, chuckling.

She places the shears on the tabletop near the cauldron, before embracing me in a tight hug. She's not much taller than I am, but she's always given the best, most firm hugs. The kind that makes you feel protected, safe, and loved. I relax into her arms, returning the squeeze happily. My dad strides over to the two of us, wrapping his much longer arms around both of us.

"We knew you could do it, kiddo," his voice rumbles through the embrace.

My parents squeeze me tight one more time before we finally break apart. My mom swipes a few errant tears from her cheeks, then gives a self-deprecating laugh. "Oh, my little girl is all grown-up. I'm so proud of you. We both are," she says, her eyes sliding from my face to my dad's.

He nods when I glance at him, "We're both so proud of you, kiddo."

As if he's upset over being forgotten, the toad I created releases a long, deep, belch-sounding croak. The three of us laugh, the noise relieving some sappiness our family hug created.

"What do I do with animals from potions?" I ask. Prior to his croak, I hadn't thought about the toad's fate after being magicked into existence.

"You can release them into the wild, if they're native creatures that can survive the climate" my dad says. "If they're not... well it gets more complicated. When I was younger, about your age, I had to drive to the Portland Zoo and tell them I found a wandering penguin, after I brewed a potion without thinking of the outcome."

"What did they say?" I ask, amused.

My dad thinks for a second before he replies, "I can't remember their exact wording, but it was clear they thought I bought him from an exotic pet dealer or something. At least they didn't call the police," he says.

"I think we should keep the toad. We can buy an aquarium to commemorate your first success," my mom interjects excitedly.

My dad and I exchange a glance. "Mom, I don't think we need a toad in the house—" I start.

At the same time my dad says, "Jacob wouldn't want to take care of a toad, dear—"

We both stop mid-sentence. Our gray eyes connect and we chuckle.

Throwing her hands in the air, my mom relents, "Fine. We can release him in the wild. But don't come to me disappointed when you wish you'd kept your first toad!"

"I don't think I'll regret not keeping an amphibian as a trophy, Mom. Besides, I bottled a second vial of the potion. So, if I ever become nostalgic, I can relive the experience." I raise the vial of pale-yellow liquid to show her.

"Oh, we should put that somewhere special!" my mom exclaims. "Where can we put this, so we can show guests?" She turns to my dad, looking for guidance.

He looks at me with a quirked brow, and I give a quick shake of my head. I've always had a special bond with my parents, but I'm more like my dad. He's usually able to tell what I'm thinking from a single expression.

In a gentle tone, my dad suggests, "Why don't we keep it down here on a shelf? That way it's ready for Mira to use if she decides to, and it won't accidentally get lost, or broken."

"Oh, okay. That's an excellent idea." My mom agrees. She picks up the vial and strides across the room. She makes a small space on a shelf between some knick-knacks and gently places my potion in the cleared area. "Here we go," she says happily.

"Thanks mom," I reply with a slight grin. "And thanks for coming down here ready to defend me. I'm going to go upstairs and call Sylvia."

My parents both nod and wrap their arms around each other as they watch me bound exit the witching chamber.

I bound up the stairs and down the hall, dialing Sylvia's number the second my door shuts. My phone rings until it hits voicemail. "Hi, you've reached Sylvia A. Leave a message and I'll get back to you ASAP" blares through the speaker of my phone.

I decide to leave a quick message. "Hey Syl, it's Mira. I have some exciting news, call me back!" Then I hand up the phone and throw myself backwards onto my bed, disappointed she didn't answer. I stare at the ceiling for two minutes before I decide to text Leif.

He'll be proud of my accomplishment, right? It's basically "our" accomplishment, anyway. Without his help, I may have never made a successful potion.

I write out a few messages. Rereading then deleting each one until I finally settle on: **I did it!!**

His response is almost immediate: **I knew you could! What did you brew?**

I smile and type back: **A toad summoner!!**

The three dots appear on my phone, signifying Leif is typing a response. They stay on my screen for a moment before disappearing. I keep my phone in my hand for another couple minutes, watching the screen, and waiting for him to reply.

At the five-minute mark, I drop my phone to the bed next to me with a sigh. I'm bummed he cut our conversation short, but I guess he's busy and will respond later.

My gaze drifts back towards the ceiling as my thoughts wander. I'm not sure how long I spend thinking before a light tap on my bedroom door startles. Bolting upright, I become slightly woozy, but I spot a blurry version of Leif leaning against my door jamb with a smirk. I'm starting to think the arrogant smile is his natural facial expression.

"Hello, Mira Love," he says in a confident tone, after a few beats of staring.

Gathering my wits and fighting my lightheadedness, I respond, "Hi, Leif Golden."

He releases a deep chuckle. "I came to ask if you'd like to go out for lunch to celebrate? My treat, of course."

"Oh," I say, startled. Looking down at myself and noticing my grubby jeans I reply, "Yeah, sure. Let me change really quickly." I rise from my bed and head to my closet. A pair of clean shorts immediately catches my eye. I grab them from the shelf, hoping the weather stays warm.

When I turn around, Leif is still leaning against the door watching me. I frown and make a shooing motion with both hands, but Leif just quirks a brow at the movement. With a huff, I stride over to the door and push him into the hall. Before I close it fully, I state, "Go wait downstairs in the entryway or something."

Leif chuckles again, but I hear his footsteps retreat down the hall towards the stairs. I quickly change and slide on a pair of sandals. Checking myself in the mirror, I tighten the ribbon in my hair, then descend the steps to meet up with Leif.

He's not waiting in the foyer like I expected. As my eyes scan the area, I catch a flash of his hair down the hall. Quietly, I creep in that direction, hoping for the chance to observe him for a second.

As I near, I hear him speaking and realize he's heard my approach. "You get your looks from your mother, eh?" Leif comments without facing me.

I stop walking on my tiptoes and stride towards Leif's tall, lanky form and the wall of pictures he's looking at. He's standing in front of a photo from a few years prior. I'm holding one of my paintings, a parent on either side, with an arm wrapped around me. They both tower over my short frame. My mother, with her heart-shaped face, and blonde hair like my own, is closer to my height, but much curvier. My dad is almost a foot taller than her with short, combed brown hair and twinkling, almond-shaped, gray eyes.

The image is from my first gallery show and seeing the photo puts a smile on my face as I recall the memory behind it. My parents submitted my painting, the one I'm holding in the picture, without my knowledge. When the submission was accepted, my mom tore through the house and into my room to show me the letter, jumping up and down with her excitement over my accomplishment.

"Yeah," I respond quietly. "I look more like my mom, but act more like my dad."

While I talk, Leif's eyes shift to my face. His expression transitions to something unrecognizable as he watches me. When I'm done speaking, he allows silence to linger. He seems to mull something over, but when he opens his mouth to speak, he simply says, "Well, why don't we go grab something to eat?"

I nod. "Yeah, let's go."

10

THE GIFT

Mirabella

With a smile, I open my door and wait for Leif to round the car. Together we head through the entry of the chrome and glass Diner, and my stomach rumbles in anticipation. As I approach the hostess stand, I feel like a regular. "A table for two, please."

The girl leads us to a booth in the corner and plops down two menus before striding away. I covertly watch Leif from under my lashes, wondering what he thinks of the shimmery tabletops and slightly sticky menus. He sticks his tongue out while he picks up his menu and I realize he must notice me watching.

I giggle to cover my embarrassment and quickly look over the food choices. As I set my menu on the table, Cindy appears. She pulls a pen from behind her ear and flips to a clean page of her order book. "What can I get you, sweetie?" she asks me.

"One burger with bacon and avocado. Medium, please."

Cindy nods and turns to Leif. A flash of brown appears in my peripherals and I turn interested to see what caught my eye. Time seems to slow and a ringing begins in my ears as Kaylee, Greg, and their crew walk in through the front door.

I sink further into the booth, hoping to keep out of sight. Simultaneously, I start a chant in my head. *Seat them across the Diner. Seat them across the Diner. Seat them across the Diner.*

Unfortunately, the higher powers that be are not listening to my pleading words. From my crouched position, I timidly watch as the hostess gathers menus and leads the group of eight closer and closer to my table with Leif.

The hostess stops at the booth directly behind me. I can tell the second that Kaylee spots Leif. Her face turns white as a sheet, like she's seen a ghost. The hostess is about to plop the menus onto the table, but Kaylee's arm shoots out. She intercepts half of the menus, throwing the other half to the floor in her haste.

"Not this one," she says, angrily. She tears her eyes away from Leif to glare at the hostess. "Over there," she demands, pointing across the room.

When the group is finally seated in the furthest corner, I breathe a sigh of relief and sit upright again. Leif clears his throat in a suspicious way.

Moving my eyes to his face, I see he's struggling to conceal a smile. I watch as he attempts to straighten his lips several times, before successfully pulling them into a flat line. "So, a toad summoner?" He questions.

"Yes!" I exclaim, breaking into a grin. "On my first try. Thank you for helping me... I don't even feel like I did anything different, but it worked perfectly."

"I knew you could do it," Leif replies, with an answering grin. He reaches behind his back and pulls out a wrapped gift bag. One I hadn't noticed prior . Before I have a chance to question where it came from, Leif says, "I brought you a small gift."

Fighting the urge to squeal excitedly and snatch the bag like I want to, I compose myself and slowly reach across the table to take it. With practiced patience, I slowly pull the pieces of tissue paper to reach the contents underneath.

Nestled inside are three leather-bound books. I remove them one at a time. The first one is a dusky green color with the outline of a leaf on the front. I run my hand over the leather admiring the buttery-soft feeling. I place the book on the table before reaching back into the bag. The next book is a muted blue with the outline of a small pile of dust on the cover. I repeat the gesture with my hand, feeling the leather before placing it atop the first book. Placing my hand in the bag one more time, I remove the third book. This text is a dry red color with a vial on the front. Once all three of them are on the table, I place the bag on the bench next to me and look at Leif expectantly.

His brown eyes connect with mine before sliding to the pile of books. He runs a hand lightly over the cover of the top one, mimicking my movements from earlier. "Each of these explains magical ingredients and the importance of the families they belong to. The first one tells about plants and which families of plants produce which types of magic. The second explains other natural sources of magic, such as dust and soil. The third discusses magical gases and liquids. As part of your written witches exams, you'll need to identify the main magical families. These books will help us study for that and I wanted you to have your own copy for reference. If you can't find a particular ingredient, it's possible to substitute another ingredient in the same magical family. Eventually I'd like to go over all of this in-depth, but we'll start with the materials on the test first. Of course."

"Oh, wow," I exclaim softly. Pulling the book off the top of the stack, I run my hand over the cover once more before flipping to a page at random. Across the top of the page a bold header reads, "Tiger's Breath". Below the header is a sketched image of a vial with a swirling orange liquid. The page explains where the gas is found, the magical family it's from, and its various properties.

After skimming the text, my eyes meet Leif's muddy brown gaze again. "This is so great, thank you."

Leif smiles and gives a dip of his head. "I was

thinking we could schedule your exams for two weeks from now. What do you think?"

Upon registering his words, my previous elation immediately turns to dread. My hands become clammy and I clasp them in my lap to hide my slight tremor. "I just," I begin, my voice squeaking from my sudden nerves. I clear my throat and try again, "I just finished my first successful potion on my own. You don't think it's too soon? What happens if I fail?"

Leif offers a warm expression. "Mira Love, you need to have more confidence. Remember that text I showed you about your family?" I nod my head, even though he doesn't appear to be waiting for a response. "You're a legacy. Being a powerful witch is in your blood. You CAN do this. You just need to pick up a few tricks of the trade first, so to speak. But that's why I'm here. Together, we can do anything. I promise you that."

I let the confidence in his voice and words seep into my bones. I am a legacy. I can do this. It's in my blood.

The reassurances from both Leif and myself help to uncoil the nerves low in my belly and the sweat on my palms starts to dissipate. "Okay then. If you think two weeks is all the time we need to practice, I trust you." I reply.

Leif opens his mouth to reply, but he's cut off by Cindy. "Two bacon and avocado burgers, one medium and one well done?" I smile when I realize we ordered the same thing. My parents do that all the time, and I've always given them crap for not ordering two separate menu items and splitting them with each other.

A throat clearing interrupts my thoughts and I realize Cindy is waiting for me to clear the table so she can put our plates down. After a brief shuffle, I place the tissue paper and books back into the gift bag from Leif. Cindy distributes the burgers and returns to the kitchen.

As I'm lifting my juicy burger to my mouth, ready to take a bite, Leif finally finishes his thought from earlier. "After we eat, we should probably get to studying. We're going to be spending a lot of time together, Mira Love."

With my mouth full, I nod in response. When I finish chewing my bite, I ask Leif the question I've had since my talk with Marc. "How much do you know about the curse on the witches and the shifters?"

Leif places his burger back down on his plate and wipes his fingers on a napkin politely draped across his lap. Clearing his throat, he replies, "From what I've heard, it all started with a spring."

"A spring?" I ask, taken aback.

Leif nods, rather vigorously. "Yes. The shifters found a spring they believed contained magical properties. They thought that it could heal their sicknesses and extend their lives."

My eyes widen at his words. This is unlike the other two stories that I've heard regarding the curse. Already engrossed, I make the universal motion for "please continue", as I pick up my burger for another bite.

"The witches heard of the spring, and asked the wolves for permission to use it. The shifters laughed at the coven, saying it was for shifters only. They said the witches could make their own magic water if they needed it so badly. One day, out of spite, a younger witch in the coven saw a trio of wolves headed to the spring. One of the shifters was extremely ill and she used the distraction to follow behind them undetected. She hid and waited until they left, then attempted a very difficult curse on her own."

"She tried to curse the wolves." I interject, predicting the direction of his story.

"No," Leif denies, to my surprise. "She attempted to steal the magic from the spring and bottle it for her own use. She saw the wolves use the spring and was jealous of their resource."

"What happened next?" I ask, completely enthralled.

Leif sighs. "The spell was executed poorly and something went terribly wrong. Somehow the spring dried up. Shifters were cursed to follow the call of their wolf, and witches were stripped of all of their magic except for potions. Some witches say it was a punishment from the forces of the earth, some say it was the cost of the curse, others state it was the result of a magical backfire." Leif shrugs and picks up his burger.

I sit there thinking over his words and losing my appetite. How are there so many versions of the curse?

And how am I supposed to find a cure and help Vlad if no one actually knows what happened?

Another question forms while I mull over Leif's tale. "Was this spring in Florence?"

Shaking his head, Leif talks around a mouthful of food. "Somewhere in Canada."

AT ALMOST MIDNIGHT, I fall face down onto my bed, exhausted. Leif wasn't kidding about studying or spending a lot of time together. After the Diner, he helped me to create flashcards for the basic plants, dusts, gases, and liquids used in potion brewing. Then he spent hours quizzing and correcting me, until the only thoughts left in my brain were ones about magical ingredients.

My phone buzzes in my pocket, waking me from my hazy, almost sleep that started as soon as my eyes were shut. I use my left hand to retrieve it, then prop myself up on both elbows to see who's texting me so late at night. Sylvia's name is a notification on my screen, followed by Leif's.

I click open Leif's text first: **Sleep Well, Mira Love. I'll be over tomorrow for another practice session. Will bring coffee.**

I type out a quick response: **Sounds good. See you then.**

Then I click over to Sylvia's name. Her message is actually three separate messages about different topics:

O M G. Who do you think left the note? Are you avoiding Leif now?

And your first potion on your own????? My little Mira is all grown up!

Also, sorry today was so crazy. School was a mess, then family drama. I had like NO time all day. Can I come over tomorrow to catch up?

Whenever Sylvia texts me, I hear her tone in my head through the message. These oscillate between skeptical, ecstatic, annoyed, then back to her normal, calmer tone.

I message her back quickly: **It was a crazy day for me too. I have a lot to tell you... can you come over early? Leif and I are going to study more for the written exam!**

Sylvia sends back a bunch of emojis including a face with heart eyes, a shocked face, and a thumbs up.

I send another quick message to Leif: **Can we do eleven or later? Sylvia is stopping by in the morning!**

I don't wait for a reply. If he doesn't see the message tonight, he'll see it tomorrow before he heads over. He'll get the message in time, so it's not worth delaying sleep any longer.

I place my phone on the nightstand, then change into my pajamas, and climb back in bed. Despite being ready to pass out only ten minutes prior, I'm suddenly wide awake. Like my brief text messaging stint activated my brain again.

While I lay there willing sleep to come, I realize

thoughts of Vlad, his whereabouts and overall well-being, have barely crossed my mind over the past few days. I'm plagued by guilt almost immediately. I feel like a terrible friend, or maybe a terrible girlfriend. I'm not really sure which, since we didn't classify our relationship prior to his disappearance. Either way, I haven't spent much time trying to find him since Leif barged into my life.

Jumping out of bed, I run to my closet and throw open the doors. Without bothering to flip on the light, I dig around on the top shelf for a few minutes. I continue until my right hand hits the piece of fabric I'm seeking. I pull out Vlad's sweatshirt and slip the bulky piece of fabric over my head, inhaling deeply as it passes my face. Vlad's scent wafts up, his earthy, musky smell teasing my nostrils with each breath.

With a sigh, I crawl back into bed and snuggle my face in the sweatshirt's neck. Inhaling deeply, I breathe in the soothing smell of pine trees and ocean water. I think of Vlad and what life will be like, when he finally returns from wherever he is. Within seconds, I fall asleep.

11

THE OFFER

Mirabella

Sylvia appears on my doorstep bright and early bearing a breakfast burrito and a coffee that's more sugar than caffeine. With a smile, I invite her in and we wordlessly enter my studio. I unravel the wrapper covering my burrito and take a huge bite as we settle into the leather chairs. The bacon-y, cheese-y goodness hits my tongue and I let out an mmm in appreciation. "Will you bring me a burrito every day?" I ask Sylvia.

She laughs. "I'm sure you could have these made here daily, if you asked for it."

"It's not the same," I mumble around a mouthful of food.

Sylvia allows me a few more bites before pestering me for information. "So, you're still spending time with

Leif even after that creepy note someone left on your porch?"

Swallowing the last bit of my burrito, I follow with a sip of my coffee, then I'm ready for this conversation. "Well, really the note warned me to be cautious... not to avoid Leif. He's honestly been a ton of help so far."

Sylvia hmms, but doesn't reply other than that.

I continue, feeling the need to justify my decision considering her wariness. "There hasn't been any weirdness after the Kaylee incident either."

We sit in silence for a few seconds. I watch Sylvia's face as she thinks about the meaning of the weird note and Leif's intentions. I remain frozen, not wanting to disturb her thinking process. Sylvia's opinion is important to me.

Since Leif arrived, I've had a tiny niggle in the back of my mind that he isn't here for completely selfless reasons. It makes it hard for me to trust that he has good intentions.

Sylvia opens her mouth to reply, but is interrupted by a knock on the doorframe. I see her eyes widen before both of our heads whip to the door to see who may have been eavesdropping.

Jacob offers a close-lipped smile, dipping his head. "Sorry to interrupt Miss Love, Miss Amica," he says addressing both Sylvia and I. "A Mr. Golden is downstairs, waiting in the entry."

My brow furrows, and I remove my phone from my pocket to check the time and any missed messages.

The clock on the front screen shows 8:30 and no notifications. I exchange glances with Sylvia.

Leif is early, super early, despite my request for him to show up closer to midday.

"Sorry, he wasn't supposed to be here for a few more hours," I apologize.

Sylvia shrugs, "Well, I guess we could both help you study. We can talk more later, after he leaves."

"Sorry Syl," I say with a grimace. "I asked him to come over at eleven. I'm not sure why he's so early."

With a smile that looks a little forced, she replies, "Let's go see what your boy wants."

Feeling guilty for not being able to dedicate more time to Sylvia, although at no fault of my own, I return the smile. "He's not my boy, but let's go see if he has a good reason for being so early. If not, we can kick him out so we can finish catching up."

Sylvia rises from her seat, following me out the door. "Yeah right, he'd probably turn me into a frog or something for threatening him."

I HAVE a feeling of deja vu, as Sylvia sits in an armchair. She's crunching on snacks while Leif and I stand by the cauldron running through our flashcards for the third time. The only difference between this study session versus the last one, is my two separate coffee beverages.

Once we finish reviewing the final card, Leif mixes

them up for another go. I turn to Sylvia. "How did you prepare for the witches exams?"

She crunches through the rest of her chip then responds, "My dad made a study guide of things I needed to know and a list of reference books. He let me loose in the family library to find the information and study. That was when I was fifteen though, so I had an advantage of years of study... instead of weeks like you."

I nod and ignore the slightly apologetic look on her face.

Whenever Sylvia's knowledge of witches comes up, she always looks regretful. I chalk it up to her knowing we were witches without telling me, but I never acknowledge it. We moved past that point in our friendship. I'm over it and eventually she will be too.

Leif interjects, "Typically that's how the process works." He continues to shuffle the cards, his hands slowing once he realizes he's garnered our attention.

"What do you mean typically works like that?" I ask.

Shrugging, Leif places the cards back on the table. "The Coven usually designates a specific person to train each new witch. Some take a more hands-off approach like Sylvia's dad. Some trainers spend more time working together, like we are."

"What age do most witches start studying?" Sylvia chimes in.

Leif gives another shrug, looking at Sylvia nestled in her armchair. "It just depends on the witch and the

Coven. I wouldn't say there's a set standard. Although waiting until eighteen to learn about magic seems a bit old, if you ask me."

Neither of us ask further questions and Leif picks the flashcards back up. His shuffling is the only noise in the room until Sylvia resumes crunching on chips and scrolling through her phone.

Personally, I'm impressed she's been able to look through LifeNovel without yelling angry comments at the screen while fighting with internet strangers. Either she's growing up or she's not that comfortable around Leif to show her true colors, yet.

Out of the corner of my eye, I see her fingers rapidly fly across the screen of her phone. Her expression changes several times before she sees me watching. "Hey, my parents are asking me to come back home and watch my little brothers." She pulls a grimace. "Do you want to have dinner together tomorrow night? ...we can finish catching up." Her eyes slide pointedly to Leif, like she's silently adding "alone".

Thankfully, he's concentrating on reading something from a book we've been using to study and doesn't notice.

"Yeah, I'd like that." I walk over to the armchair and give her a quick hug. "Thanks for coming over and bringing the sustenance," I say. "Do you want me to walk you out?"

Sylvia smiles and brushes me off gently as we wander to the large wooden door together. "Nah, I know the way. Don't study too hard. And I'll see you tomorrow." Looking past me, she gives a quick wave. "Bye, Leif."

He calls out, "Goodbye." Once the door closes firmly behind her, he moves towards the armchairs. "Would it be okay if we sat for a bit?" He asks.

"Oh, of course." I nod abruptly before plopping into a chair.

Leif sits gingerly like his legs are sore and I realize we've been standing on the hard, stone floor for a few hours now. During my first few days in the witching chamber, my feet were more tender after a couple hours of working, but they desensitized to the uncomfortable feeling.

A small tendril of guilt tries to sneak in, saying I should have offered to take a break and sit sooner, but I push the thought away. After my talk with Leif at the Diner about being a legacy and needing to have confidence, I've been trying to take less accountability for other's actions, as well. Leif is an adult. He could've sat on his own, without my permission or invitation, if he needed to. End of story.

Leif interrupts my wayward thoughts. "I've been thinking, Mira Love."

He looks at me expectantly, while I stare blankly back. "Oh, and what have you been thinking about?" I ask, confused by the random statement.

"Well, I'm glad you asked." Leif says with a smirk, like he didn't introduce the topic. He leans forward, across the arm of his chair and grabs both of my hands with his. I experience a brief shock against my skin, but his words quickly override the initial surprise. "I've been thinking I would like you to come back with me. To Canada. To my coven."

I give him my best "well, duh" look. "I was already planning to do that. My grandma, Vlad, and I were all planning to do that.' I respond firmly. "When my grandma went to your coven for help, your father offered assistance, once I receive my witching license."

Leif shakes his head and gives my hands a tight squeeze. "No, I'm not interested in you coming to visit, Mira Love. I want you to come stay with me, with my coven. At least for a little while to test it out and determine if it's somewhere you would be comfortable."

I shake my head, but Leif ignores it. "We could work on strengthening your potion brewing, try pushing your limits. And we could also brew together..." He pauses, his gaze moving from the fireplace to ping back and forth between my eyes. "We're both legacy witches. Together we could brew any potion, nothing would be out of reach for us."

I slowly mull over his words, letting his idea fill my brain completely before responding. "Leif..." I begin slowly. "I really appreciate your offer. I do." He makes a scoffing noise, apparently anticipating my response. "I just don't want to leave Florence. This is my home. My family is here. Sylvia is here. And I've been seeing someone that I don't want to leave."

Leif scoffs again and his grip on my hands squeezes

tighter, bordering painful. "Seeing someone? I haven't seen anyone."

His words and attitude hit a nerve. Pulling my hands away, I place them into my lap and fold them together. Then I lean back and level an annoyed look at Leif. Despite not owing him an explanation for my decision, I give him one. "He's been going through some things and is out of town right now. I really appreciate your offer, Leif. And that your family is willing to help me. Both by sending you here and allowing me to come visit after I receive my witching license. I am very grateful, but I don't think I'm willing to completely uproot my life at this point."

I pacify him with my next statement. "Over the next couple weeks while we're studying, I'll think over your offer. I'll give you my final decision after I pass my witches exams."

My last few words seem to change Leif's attitude about the entire conversation. His signature smirk slides into place and his next words are filled with confidence. "I guess I'll just have to spend our days convincing you on the Canadian Coven, eh?"

I LEAN against the railing to my balcony, watching the rain drizzle down outside. A ringing from my room startles me from my thoughts. Hustling in through the French doors, I dig in my bedding until my hand hits the cool glass surface of my phone.

Crowing out my success, I answer without checking the caller ID. "Hello," I wheeze.

"Hello Dear," my grandma replies.

"Grandma, is everything okay?" I ask, concerned about her late-night call.

"Its... fine, dear. Well I'm fine." She starts slowly. I settle into my bed, pulling a blanket over my lap. Knowing my grandma, if this news is the least bit interesting, she's going to take her sweet time telling me.

Her pause lengthens and I ask, "What's going on?"

A sigh comes through the phone. "I had a run-in with one of the council members today." I can't help the sharp inhale of breath that follows her statement. Before I can ask her to elaborate, she continues, "Nothing happened to me. He just was very persistent for information. He wanted to know what else we've found about the curse."

"What did you tell him?" I ask. To my knowledge, we don't know any more than we did a month ago.

"I said we're working as fast as we can to uncover answers and help everyone in town." She sighs through the phone again. "I'm worried they'll become more aggressive for information soon. Something has them scared. Maybe the wolves are turning faster, without being able to shift back. We need to continue looking for answers, while being mindful of the Council."

I think over her words, playing them on repeat through my mind. "It'll be okay, right? My exams are scheduled for two weeks from today. After that, you and I can go with Leif to his coven. They should be able to help us find some answers. We'll be fine if we stay out of their sights for the next two weeks, Right?" I ask timidly.

My grandma hesitates for a moment. Silence fills the phone, which concerns me more than any answer she could have provided. When she finally speaks, it's softer than before. "Yes, dear. You're probably right. Soon we'll be able to help them find the answers they seek."

12

THE COUNTDOWN

Mirabella

Over the next few days, I barely have time to sleep between my studies with Leif, my new, shorter hours at the Daily, and carving out a little bit of time for my parents and Sylvia. When my alarm goes off on Wednesday morning, I groan loudly.

On my third attempt, I'm able to fully open my sleep-crusted eyes and swing my legs over the edge of my bed to prepare for the day. I plod through my room, gathering my long hair into a loose ponytail. I drag jeans over my legs and tug on a nice, royal blue top with flutter sleeves. Groggily, I pull on my sandals and head out the door to my Prius.

My sleep deprived brain barely registers the drive to the Daily. When I arrive, I run my hands across my face a few times in an attempt to wake up before I get out of my car.

Despite my initial resistance to Leif's highhanded actions, I'm grateful he went over my head to speak with Marc and coordinate a shorter work week for me. Even my three days of work this week have been a struggle, after long nights of cramming for my upcoming tests.

I'm the last one to pull a chair to the morning meeting, and I place myself at the back of the group. In my effort to focus I squint my eyes and try to follow the suggestions being added to the board and Marc's feedback. I allow my eyes drift shut and just listen for one brief second.

"Mira." My shoulder shakes and I grumble. "Mira," a laughing voice says again.

Prying my eyes open slowly, I see Marc's emerald gaze hovering in front of me. His eyes are twinkling like he's in on a joke I haven't heard yet.

I glance around and realize I'm the only one at the front of the room. Startled, I sit up straighter, trying to figure out what's going on. The movement pulls my shirt tighter against my shoulder and I realize the fabric is damp. I look down and see a small, circular wet spot.

Raising my hand to my face, I touch my upper cheek trying to identify the source of the liquid. Unfortunately, the part of my face that's wet is my lower chin, leading me to suspect that drool caused the dampness. "What happened?" I mumble.

My suspicion is confirmed when Marc quickly turns his face and lets out a cough that basically sounds like a laugh. When he faces me again, his expression is mostly neutral, minus the twinkle in his eyes and the upturned corner of his lips. He clears his throat twice. "You fell asleep during the morning meeting," he finally responds.

My cheeks heat with embarrassment at his revelation. "I'm so sorry, Marc," I say softly. "I've been up late cramming every night. My exams are scheduled for ten days from now..." I trail off as Marc's expression transitions from amused to annoyed.

"Why didn't you say anything?" He asks, sounding irritated.

"About my exams?"

Marc shakes his head. "About the Daily being too much for you. You can take the days off to study, Mira. You don't need to spread yourself so thin that you're falling asleep at work."

"Oh, I just didn't want to leave you short staffed..." I begin.

"You're fine Mira." Marc straightens in front of me and offers his hand to help me up from my chair. "Why don't you head home and catch up on some rest? And take next week off. You can come back once you've passed your exams."

Too tired to protest, I drag my chair back to my desk and leave the Daily without another word. Though Marc wasn't angry I fell asleep, it's still embarrassing to be the intern that drooled all over herself during the morning meeting.

When I start my car, I see it's only 7:30am. I was barely at work and spent almost my entire time there asleep. With a groan, I drive back home. I'm embarrassed, but also grateful to catch up on some rest before Leif's visit this afternoon.

A FEW HOURS LATER, a knock on my door wakes me from a deep sleep. I groggily lift my face from my pillows to examine my surroundings. Familiar furniture slowly comes into focus and registers in my foggy brain.

It takes another minute for me to peel myself from my bed and stumble towards my door. Still bogged down by the last vestiges of my deep sleep, I open the door to reveal Leif standing on the other side.

"Leif," I state, my brain working in overdrive to wake up.

He laughs and leans towards me. Before I can react, he bends over and places a soft kiss on my cheek. He whispers, "You're cute when you've just woken up."

Leif takes two steps back as I process his words. I glance down to find Vlad's oversized sweatshirt and the pair of pajama shorts I threw on from the floor. When my gaze returns to Leif's face, he's staring at my bare legs.

I clear my throat and his muddy brown gaze flies to mine. "Is it time to study already?" I ask.

"Yes, it is," Leif confirms. "I brought coffee and donuts for us. I'll wait for you downstairs, near the cauldron, while you get ready."

I firmly close the door then slip back into the jeans and top that I wore to work. In the bathroom, I quickly finger comb the strands of my ponytail before splashing my face with water. My mind is slowly, slowly starting to wake up by the time my feet hit the first stone step leading to the witching chamber.

I descend cautiously, pausing when I reach the door. Every day I see Leif, I stress about him wanting to discuss his offer further. I fear if I decline again, he'll stop helping me prepare for the exams.

Although I'm more confident in my abilities than I was before, I don't think I'm at the point of passing, yet. No one has told me the consequences, if I were to fail my exams. I don't want to ask again, because the outcome failure would have on our town is scary enough to think about.

Either way, I still need Leif's help and want to avoid discussions that upset him.

Sighing, I push against the door. I stride across the room, stopping short when I see the chaos Leif is creating. He has vials upon vials of ingredients placed to the side of the cauldron. Some are stacked rather precariously on top of others, due to the lack of space.

I watch as he references a book I can't see. He hops over to another shelf and pulls down an additional two vials, adding them to the mess. He flits about the room without acknowledging my presence, snagging ingredients randomly.

Finally, I can't contain my curiosity any longer and ask, "Leif, what are you doing?"

He looks up from his book and offers me an enormous grin. "We're done studying for the written portion of your exam. You've got that material down pat. Today we're brewing potions that could be on the exam. Even if they don't end up being the exact potions you need to make, they'll be structured similarly."

"Okaaay," I draw out. Gesturing to the mishmash of vials filled with ingredients, I ask, "What is with all this though?"

Leif takes a step back and eyes the counter in front of him. He chuckles then his brown eyes connect with my gray ones. "I guess this looks rather insane."

At my nod, he continues. "When you get to the brewing portion of your exam, it will be similar to this... just not so precarious." He says with another chuckle.

He rearranges the vials attempting to fit them all on the tabletop bordering the Cauldron. "The brewing portion of the test lasts an hour and fifteen minutes. This portion is timed, so it will not last longer. Although if you hurry, you could complete it in less time."

"That's good to know. But what are all these vials for?"

"Right," Leif chuckles again and strides across the

room to stand beside me. He slings an arm around my shoulder and pulls me into his side. "There will be a separate table with all of your ingredients, to the side of your cauldron. They'll be out of order like they are here," He says gesturing to the mayhem in front of us. "You'll have a twenty-minute segment to brew, with a five-minute break between each potion. During your twenty minutes, you'll have to find your ingredients on the table, brew your potion, and bottle two vials. After time is called, your proctor will test the potion. If it works, you pass that round."

Normally, the ingredients in my parents' witching chamber are in alphabetical order on the shelves surrounding the cauldron. Despite the disorder, I'm thankful Leif thought to mimic the exam in its entirety.

I would've been overwhelmed and stressed to go from such an organized way of brewing to total chaos and a limited time frame. Better to practice like this and hunt for my ingredients than to go in unprepared and risk failure.

I crane my neck to look at Leif. His attention is directed towards ingredients, but he meets my gaze when I speak. "What happens if I fail to brew a potion correctly?"

"You only have to successfully brew two of the three potions. If you fail the first two rounds, you can't continue. If you pass the first two, you have an option to brew the third or not. I would recommend brewing. Whichever Coven you end up at will appreciate a full assessment of your abilities. Including if you were able to complete all three potions successfully." He squeezes me tighter against his side at the end of his statement.

Ignoring his subtle reference to his proposition, I ask my last question, "How do you know which potions will be on the exam?"

"I don't." Leif shrugs. "But I know what types of potions will be included. Without question, each potion will contain only three ingredients. Although the ingredients used in a potion can affect the complexity, it is a general rule of thumb that a simpler potion requires fewer ingredients."

Leif turns me toward him, moving to wrap his arms loosely around my lower waist. The position feels too intimate. So I lean back, creating space between us.

He's undeterred and smiles down at me. "Don't be afraid of the exam, eh? You learned the ingredients and their uses very quickly. I'm impressed and I know you're going to kill this test. Are you ready to get started, Mira Love?"

I step back, breaking through the loop of his arms and stride to the cauldron. "I'm ready."

Leif removes a stopwatch from his pocket. "We're going to mock the regular test. I'll tell you when to start, then you'll get twenty minutes to brew. After that we'll have a five-minute period to test, clean-up, and prepare for the next round. The manual near the cauldron is open to your first potion. Are you ready?"

I glance around at the disarray surrounding me

and inhale a deep, calming breath. This is just a trial run. I can perfect any issues before the real deal. I glance at the empty, then drag my eyes upwards to connect with Leif's. We stare at each other intently for a brief minute, then I nod my head.

"Okay, go!"

13

THE EXAM

Mirabella

The coven conducts all their business matters in a large industrial style building on the outskirts of town. I'm a jumble of excited nerves as I drive towards it on the day of my witches exams. Despite my protests, I'm followed by an entourage of supporters.

Leif and Sylvia are in my car. The two of them are unknowingly mitigating some nerves as they squabble like siblings over the name of an actor for a popular TV Show. I tune them out slightly as I cautiously drive towards my test, however; I appreciate the distraction.

Checking my review mirror, I see the rest of the cars following behind me. My grandmother's ancient burgundy Chevelle is right on my bumper. Behind her at a more reasonable distance, my parents follow with the Morts in their Black SUV, the Amica family is next in line in a similar vehicle. Marc brings up the tail in his Truck.

The last addition to our group surprised me with a knock on my front door at seven in the morning. I was just finishing my third loop around the house, trying to expel all my nervous pre-test energy, prior to departure time and he invited himself.

The sight of a towering steel and brick structure snaps me from my memories of this morning. A few large, glass windows enhance the industrial appearance, glinting as the sun rises. The hulking, unsigned building is intimidating and my nerves ramp up to one thousand.

"Is this it?" I ask my now silent car. My voice is a low whisper, out of reverence or fear, I'm not sure which.

"This is it," Sylvia replies, her tone equally quiet.

I pull my Prius into the closest parking spot, waiting as the five cars following park nearby. I throw my phone into the glove box while I wait, knowing I can't bring it in for my exams.

Together Sylvia, Leif, and I open our doors and head to the front of the building. At the top of the sidewalk, I pause. Craning my neck, I look up, up, and up to the top of the building, wondering what else happens here to require such a massive space.

Leif slings his arms around my shoulders and talks quietly near my ear, "There's a lot going on in the world of witches. Potions are just the tip of the iceberg." He gives me a squeeze before dropping his arm.

Dropping my gaze, I find my family and friends have crowded around. My eyes flit from my parents, to my grandma, to the Morts minus Vlad, to the Amicas, to Marc, and finally to Leif.

"Ready?" I ask.

A chorus on nods and a few yesses sound out from the group. Together, we walk through the front door of the building and into the lobby. I'm surprised to see the interior looks serene. A large koi pond sits a couple dozen feet from the entry, fully equipped with a babbling waterfall and split down the middle with a decorative wooden bridge.

Past the pond is a bay of sleek, black elevator doors. My gaze follows the wall to the left and skims over a coffee stand before finally reaching the reception desk. It seems similar to a fancy hotel lobby, instead of the headquarters for a witch coven.

Glancing at my parents, I seek some guidance on what to do next. My mom makes a subtle shooing motion towards the reception desk. I force my feet to step one in front of the other as I approach the two women dressed in black robes.

"Hi," I croak out. Clearing my throat, I try again. "Hi, I'm Mira Love. Here for my witches exams. Could you point me in the right direction?"

Without looking up from the tablet-like device in front of her, the robed woman on the left points to the elevator. "All testing takes place on the fourth floor. Take the elevator and follow the signs."

I walk back to my crew and say, "Fourth floor." Surveying the size of the group, I tack on, "We may need two elevators."

We head to the black doors and divvy up between the two elevators that arrive within seconds of one another. As soon as the doors close, the elevator shoots up and almost immediately dings that we arrive. Leif laughs as I exit on shaky legs, feeling a sense of vertigo.

"They're spelled to be more efficient," he informs me.

"That was terrible," I groan.

A couple chuckles sound out from the group around me as I grab onto the wall for a few seconds. I cling onto the drywall, attempting to regain my balance until I feel like I can walk again.

Eventually, our little gaggle makes its way down the winding hallways, following the signs directing us towards the witches exams. It feels like half an hour before we finally reach a waiting area with other young witches and their parents.

Most of the other witches have one or two family members with them. My cheeks heat with embarrassment when I realize I'm the only one that brought a ten-person team to cheer me on.

The eight-minute wait for my test crawls by. The others waiting discreetly glance at my group periodically, but everyone seems content to keep to themselves. I notice some witches have books perched on their laps, attempting a last-minute study session.

It's an eternity before a stern looking older woman appears. She has a wrinkled face, with dark sunken eyes, and a mass of gray hair pulled into a tight bun. Like the receptionists, she's also clad in a set of dark robes. Must be a uniform for the building. Either that or witches closely affiliated with the coven all have the same fashion tastes.

She stands just outside the wooden door and claps her hands twice. The already quiet room falls silent. "Any witches here to take the exam, please form an orderly line here." She points to a square on the floor before us.

My mom pulls me into a tight embrace, passing me to my dad quickly after. Once he lets go, I'm swept up again, this time by Tricia, with Mr. Mort giving me a fatherly pat on the back.

When they let go, Sylvia rushes forward to grab my hands. She's loud and excited when she offers her encouraging words. "You can do this, Mira!" Her parents nod enthusiastically behind her.

My grandma steps up to my side, wiping a few tears away from the corner of her eyes, then gives my hand a quick squeeze. Leif gives me a one-armed hug with a side of static shock, then steps back.

Marc is the final member of my crew to wish me luck. For a second, he and I stare at each other awkwardly, before laughing and stepping forward into a warm hug. I feel the electric, tumbling, dryer feeling

I've felt when hugging him in the past, only much less intense.

We separate, and he looks down at me with an affectionate expression. "You can do this Mira. I believe in you." His eyes flit past me to the others and he adds, "We all do."

With a deep exhale, I turn back to the rest of my entourage and offer a small wave and a half smile. Then I join the line of witches waiting to take the written exam. The proctor ushers us inside the testing room and I hear a final quiet wave of murmured encouragement from my family before the door slams shut behind us.

My attention switches from my crew to the witches standing in front of me. There's eight of us in total, six females, including myself, and two males. Unsure what to do, the eight of us remain in a line at the front of the classroom. To our left sit fifteen or so desks staggered so no two are directly in line. To our right sits a teacher's desk with a blackboard centered on the wall behind it.

The proctor claps her hands together again, twice. Once it becomes clear, she plans to provide instructions from her current position standing by the door, our line awkwardly shuffles in a half circle to face her.

"Alright, we will begin the day with the written portion of your witches exams. You MUST pass this portion of the exam with at least eighty-seven percent accuracy, in order to participate in the brewing portion of the test. There will be one-hundred questions and you will have an hour to accurately answer as many as you can. The test will be a combination of multiple choice and fill in the blank, with a few true or false thrown in. If you finish early, come up to my desk. You will sit in the seat to the side while I grade your test. Your results will be provided immediately. Any questions?"

A few heads shake to decline, and the rest of the line remains mute.

"You may choose your desk," our proctor announces.

After a brief scramble, all eight of us are seated. The proctor walks around passing out exam booklets and pencils to each witch. She places the booklets face down on the desk, to provide each of us with the same amount of time.

Our proctor returns to the front and settles into the chair behind the desk. A clicking noise echoes through the room and a large, red set of numbers reading 60:00 appear on the chalkboard behind her. She's the focus of our rapt attention and seems to bask in her position of power for a second before calling out, "Begin."

The red numbers behind her count down rapidly. I immediately flip over my booklet and open to the front page. The first question is easy, multiple choice:

What is the preface for a root commonly used in sleeping spells?

A) *Dog* B) *Angel* C) *Root* D) *Somnia*

I circle D and move to the next question. That answer is easy as well. I fly through the first twenty-five multiple choice questions, my confidence growing with each answer. When I hit question twenty-six, I'm completely stumped.

Approximately ninety percent of berries used in potion brewing are toxic. True or False.

My dormant nerves flare back to life and my pencil slides around in my now clammy hand. I don't remember going over these types of facts. I quickly review all the information I remember about berries. From what I recall, at least half the berries I studied were toxic. But half isn't very close to ninety percent. I take a gamble and circle false.

After the berry question, the test returns to the expected material. I cruise through the remainder of the booklet, keeping my eyes on my work. I never look up at the clock, not wanting anxiety to choke me up, if my pace isn't quick enough.

With a deep breath, I finally close the last page of the test. I glance at the clock and notice half the other witches are already gone. The clock reads 00:05. I finished just in time.

A loud buzzing noise sounds and the numbers pulse 00:00 before disappearing from the chalkboard. "Pencils down," our proctor calls out.

She announces our names one by one, grading each test individually while the rest of us wait. I can't see exactly how the grading is accomplished from my spot near the back, but it happens rather quickly.

After five minutes of waiting, the proctor calls my name, "Mirabella Love."

I'm third, behind two witches that failed the exam. With a pit of dread in my stomach, I timidly make my way to the desk and plop my test booklet in front of the proctor for review.

She pours a silvery liquid onto the test and the majority of the pages disappear. The proctor flips through the remaining three pages before her and I see red markings on a few of the questions. "Eighty-Nine percent. You Pass. Please wait outside for the next portion of the exam."

On shaky legs, I stagger towards the doorway, pausing to take a deep breath before I exit. I passed! The second my feet touch the waiting area; my group swarms me. My parents appear to be holding their breath, as everyone else aims an anxious stare in my direction. My voice comes out louder than expected as I yell, "I passed!"

A round of cheers rises from my family, and friends gathered around me. One of the parents nearby glares and shushes loudly as she consoles a crying witch. Feeling slightly abashed, I glance around and notice all the witches that failed are still in the waiting area.

Quieter, I say, "I get to move on to the next exam."

"We're so proud of you, Kiddo," my dad says with a smile.

Marc squeezes my palm quickly and adds, "Not a single doubt that you'd pass, Mira."

Tricia interjects, "You'll ace the next test too!" Mr. Mort also nods his agreement from behind her right shoulder, his bald head glistening in the light.

As I stand in the group of my friends and family, I'm hit with a strong yearning. I wish Vlad were here, desperately. The thought deflates my prior happiness and I feel on the verge of tears.

Leif notices the change in my mood immediately. He ambles closer and slings an arm around my shoulder. For the first time, I lean into his comforting touch and watch my entourage animatedly talk to one another from the protection of his side.

14

THE SABOTAGE

Mirabella

The proctor returns, causing an immediate hush to fall over the waiting area. She allows the silence to linger for a moment, then begins, "Four witches passed the written exam. Next, we will conduct the brewing portion of the test. This is an individually conducted exam. You will take the test alphabetically, one at a time. Family and friends may access the viewing platform from the door, there." She points to an unmarked door.

She strides across the room to another wooden door and opens it. "Maximus Kire, you are first."

"At least you're probably next," Leif whispers into my ear as a nervous-looking guy makes his way towards the open door.

"That's true," I whisper back, appreciating his support.

My cluster of family and friends wander over to the benches lining the wall. I sit with them occasionally interjecting comments, but mostly, I'm distracted. My palms are sweaty and my brain feels like it's short circuiting. Time appears to slow as I wait for the boy ahead of me to complete his test.

When the boy returns. I clench my palms together, praying to hear my name next.

"Mirabella Love," the proctor announces.

As I rise to my feet, I feel as if I'm treading water, attempting to stay afloat in a sea of anxiety. My group smiles encouragingly as they also rise from the bench and file through the door to the observation platform. Their faces blur as they pass, and I barely stop myself from calling out to my mom.

Slowly, my legs carry me across the room, past a silently weeping Maximus Kire. I avert my gaze, forcing my spine to straighten and my knees to lift as I pass. I can't focus on failing or dwell on Maximus right now.

The proctor consults a scroll as I step up to the entryway. "Mirabella Love?" She asks in a calm, but stern voice.

I nod, wordlessly. I couldn't respond even if I wanted to. My throat is dry and my mouth feels stuffed full of cotton.

"Follow me, then." She says with a curt dip of her head.

Her black robes swish as she turns and enters the testing chamber. I follow closely behind, eyes flitting about as we walk into an enormous but mostly empty, square room with a vaulted ceiling. My gaze shifts upwards, hoping to catch sight of my entourage, however there is only a wall of mirrors up above. Although I can't see through, I give a quick wave to my family and friends behind the glass.

The walk across the stone floor passes quickly. Before long, the proctor stops in front of a sizable pewter cauldron settled atop a sturdy, wooden table. The ground directly to the left of the table is charred. A perfect circle is imprinted in a deep black chalky substance, as if an inferno recently occurred.

Dragging my eyes away from the spot, my gaze lands on a table filled with ingredients. Rows upon rows of vials are crammed onto the surface in a mishmash, much like the chaos Leif created in my parent's witching chamber. Not for the first time, I'm grateful for his forethought in preparing me for my exams.

"Miss Love?" My proctor asks, pulling my attention away from the tables. I meet her gaze and she quickly explains the exam structure. "When you have completed your potion, you must place the vial on that small wooden table." She points to the center of the room. "This signifies that you are finished and stops the timer," she concludes. "Do you have any questions?"

"Err, no. I don't think so," I reply, lacking confidence.

She raises a single brow, but doesn't comment. She

simply states, "Then you may stand behind the cauldron."

I position myself on the far side of the table, facing the center of the room. The second my feet stop moving, my proctor speaks again, "Your time begins now." Her words are accompanied by a click which produces a large timer. The display projects across the far wall, showing 20:00.

I force my eyes away as the time hits 19:48. The potions manual is open already, and my eyes skim the ingredients quickly, repeating the words in my head: blancara leaves, devil's root, moon dust.

Over and over, I repeat the names as I move to the ingredient table and skim over vials. I locate the blancara leaves almost immediately, confirming with the label twice before adding the vial to the main table and giving myself an internal fist bump.

I continue to repeat the two remaining ingredients, devil's root and moon dust, as my eyes search for their vials. Moon dust is a sparkling blue-white powder. The distinct substance catches my eye next and I retrieve it, placing the vial near the cauldron.

Releasing a long exhale, I search for the last and most difficult to find ingredient: devil's root. Devil's root is a plain, light-brown root, one that looks similar to at least ten other roots. My eyes flit from each root reading the labels until they hit the last one displaying "devil's root". I pick up the vial, but instead of feeling victorious, I feel like something's wrong. I study the root and the label for a solid thirty seconds before putting it back down.

My hand is immediately drawn to another vial containing a root. I pick it up and see the label says "dog root". The color is the exact same, but for some reason this vial feels "right" when the other one, the one with the correct label, did not.

Do I go with my gut and use the ingredient that feels right? Or use the one that feels wrong?

Glancing at the clock, I see the timer is at 16:23. Not wanting to waste any more time, I go with my gut and grab the vial labeled with the "wrong" ingredient. If the potion doesn't brew the way it's supposed to, I have two more attempts. If I pass both, I can still pass the entire exam.

Decision made; I hurry to my cauldron and start brewing. I pour in water from a bucket off to the side and bring the liquid to a boil. While the cauldron heats, I read the potion instructions three more times until I can recite the measurements by heart.

I stir the water three times, then remove three leaves from the vial, crushing them in my hand before throwing them into the bubbling water. The cauldron hisses as the leaves hit the bottom.

Next, I take the "dog root" and cut off three one-inch pieces. Stirring the contents of the cauldron again, I throw in the pieces of root. A large cracking noise echoes across the room, like the sound a tree would make if struck by lightning. The sound evokes a flinch and causes me to take a half-step back, but I quickly recover.

Wiping my slightly clammy hands down my pants, wicking off all the moisture, I stir the cauldron one time, then reach into the moon dust and add one pinch to my concoction. The cauldron emits a puff of smoke as the last ingredient hits the mixture.

Taking a deep breath and sending a small prayer, I stir counterclockwise seven times as denoted in the instructions. I glance up at the clock. 12:52. When the mixture stops swirling in the cauldron, I ladle a scoop of the potion, pouring some into two vials.

With an outward calm I don't feel, I walk to the center of the room and place the completed potion on the table. The timer immediately stops counting down. A large, red 9:43 remains projected onto the wall.

My proctor steps forward, her black robes swirling around her feet with each step. She removes a vial from the table and tips it towards the floor. Instead of shattering the glass, like I've been doing at home, she allows five drops of the liquid to hit the floor, then returns the vial to the table. Before the glass completely touches the wood surface, a small snow flurry falls on us.

I look up in awe. I made it snow. Inside!

"Very good, Miss Love." My proctor states in her stern tone. "You will have five minutes before your next potion. We'll clean your cauldron while you wait." As she speaks, she pulls a vial out of her robes and drips five droplets onto the ground in the exact place she poured my potion. The liquid sizzles and the flurry of snow immediately ceases.

A few additional adults, also clad in black robes, join us in the room and disappear with the cauldron. Presumably to empty it. I stand to the side, trying to stay out of the way but fascinated by seeing witches at work.

Even though I know magic exists, it's still not a regular part of my life yet. Every time I see it happen; I get giddy like the day I learned it exists.

The five-minute respite passes by faster than a normal forty-five second period.

"Are you ready, Miss Love?" My proctor asks when the timer on the wall hits 0:00.

With a deep inhale, I round the table and return to my cauldron. After my nod, the timer is reset back to 20:00.

15

THE CELEBRATION

Mirabella

When I leave the exam room, I am entirely drained. A pounding headache pulses consistently against my skull, caused by my intense concentration on scrawling text and bubbling liquids. Despite my exhaustion, I float towards my family and friends with a warm happiness infusing my veins.

I, Mira Love, am a licensed witch.

Within seconds of entering the waiting room, I'm swarmed. The groups tentatively excited expressions blur together as everyone clamors for my attention.

"Did you pass?"

"Did she pass?"

"It looked like she passed."

"Mira, dear, are you okay?"

"Why does she look so pale?"

"Probably too much magic all at once she's not used to it."

"Should we ask the Proctor?"

"Did she pass?"

Inhaling deeply, I interject, "I passed!"

A raucous cheer rises from the group and I'm passed between bodies offering hugs. As I'm being twirled around, an angry parent shushes our group.

My mom giggles, then whispers, "Let's get out of this place before they forcibly remove us. You're all invited to come over and celebrate!"

Somehow, my car is the last to arrive at my house. Leif, Sylvia, and I clamber out of my Prius and trek up the steep drive to join the adults at my impromptu party. Sylvia strides through the door first. But before I'm able to join her, Leif catches my upper arm.

"Hold on for a second." He sticks his hand into his pocket and retrieves a small, square, red velvet box. "I bought you a gift for passing your witches exams."

"You didn't even know I was going to pass!" I exclaim.

"I have faith in you, Mira Love. There was no doubt in my mind you would pass. I'm confident in your magical abilities, even if you aren't." He takes my hand and forces my palm open, placing the small box inside.

Once he releases me, I give him a look. "You didn't need to get me anything."

"But I did anyway. Just open it. Then we can join

your party." He gestures at the box in my hand impatiently.

I relent, gasping when the contents are revealed. Nestled inside the box is a small pewter cauldron on a delicate chain. Inside the cauldron is some type of smoky stone. Moving the box from left to right, the stone refracts the light and appears to be bubbling.

"Wow, Leif, this is so beautiful. Thank you." Dragging my eyes from the necklace to meet his gaze, I find a slightly vulnerable expression on his face.

"Can I put it on you?" he asks shyly.

Turning around in response, I face away from Leif, gathering my long blonde hair into a ponytail with my hand. He gingerly fastens the clasp.

As I pivot around. I gently stroke the necklace twice, admiring the smooth feel of the metal. Our gazes lock and I ask, "How does it look?"

"Beautiful," he comments, keeping his eyes on mine.

"Hey Leif," I start hesitantly.

"Yes, Mira Love," he replies instantly.

Unsure of how to continue, I waiver for a second then blurt, "During the brewing portion of your witches exams, were some ingredients mislabeled? Like as a trick or part of the test."

Leif's eyes widen, then his brow furrows. It's clear he wasn't expecting my question. "No. As far as I'm aware, a coven would never mix up the ingredients for novice witches to test with. It's not a genuine test of knowledge if they provide misleading information. Not to mention it's extremely dangerous to mix random ingredients."

I nod. "That's what I thought."

"Then why did you ask?" Leif prods.

Twisting my lips, I consider whether I'm comfortable telling Leif my suspicions when I'm not exactly sure what happened. After a quick consideration of everything he's helped with, I decide he's a good sounding board. "When I was testing, ingredients were mislabeled.... It felt almost like sabotage."

"How so?"

"Well, for each potion I brewed, at least one ingredient had an incorrect label. And the ingredient inside the vial was very similar in appearance to the one required."

"How did you know which ingredient was the correct ingredient, if the labels weren't accurate?" He asks, pinning me with his intense gaze, his brow still furrowed.

I think back to the exam and the intuition that led me to my choices. "I just had a... hunch they weren't the correct ingredients."

Leif's eyebrows jump upwards. "A hunch?"

"Yeah, like an intuition they weren't what I needed. Then a gut feeling helped me find the correct ingredients."

"Hmm," Leif says, reminding me momentarily of Sylvia. "Well, I've never heard of the Coven sabotaging a witch during their witches exams. Or a witch relying on intuition to find the proper ingredients for their potions."

I open my mouth to retort, but Leif continues, "Honestly, there are a few possibilities. The witch before you didn't pass. It's possible he was very distraught. If he cleaned up ingredients, he could have placed them into the wrong vials accidentally. Did you use the ingredients in the vials with the correct labels?"

I shake my head no.

"Well, it's possible that they put the same ingredients in multiple vials, if the real ingredients looked alike. That would keep witches from failing if they just quickly grabbed something without reading the label." He pauses and rubs a hand over his chin and averts his eyes, as if deep in thought. "It's hard to say what happened, but I doubt it was sabotage, Mira Love." His eyes lock back onto mine.

I nod in response, keeping my lips sealed tight. I don't know what to think at this point. I guess his explanations make sense, and there is no real reason anyone in the coven would want to sabotage me. I need to talk to my grandma about this later, but I table the topic for now.

Instead, I smile at Leif and point to the door. "Should we?"

Leif shakes his head. "Just a second. Before we join the party, I wanted to ask: have you thought anymore about my offer?"

A pang of guilt hits. Leif is different than I expected. He's actually quite sweet. I appreciate his thoughtful gestures, but he feels more like my big brother than someone I'm interested in dating or living with for that matter.

"Leif," I sigh. "I appreciate all your help, I truly do. I don't think I could have passed my witches exams without you. Thank you for offering, but I need to decline. If anything changes, I'll let you know. At this time, my heart and life are in Florence."

Leif's eyes harden and his lips flatten from his typical smirk, but he dips his head in silent acknowledgement.

"Why don't we go inside and enjoy my party?"

He exhales deeply. The movement seems to release some anger and his signature smirk reappears. "This may be the last time we see each other, Mira Love. Let's make it count."

"I'll see you when I'm in Canada to visit your coven!" I retort.

Leif ignores my statement and wordlessly makes a go-ahead motion. I step past him, through the doorway, and gasp.

Jacob must have spent all day decorating the house in our absence. The entryway is filled with dozens of balloons, streamers, and a massive banner that reads, "Congratulations Mira!"

The decorations line the hall, and I follow the trail to the kitchen. Our marble countertops are piled with treats, including a plastic Halloween cauldron with steam rolling out. I step closer, inspecting the witch hat, sugar cookies and "broomsticks" made of pretzels and strings of licorice. I laugh aloud, all while appreciating my mom's effort to celebrate.

When I step back, I realize the room is strangely empty and I glance around wondering where everyone is. A few seconds later, a loud roar of laughter reaches my ears, sounding like it's coming from the living room.

I follow the noise with Leif trailing behind me, stopping in my tracks the second I reach the doorway. Leif bumps into my back but doesn't apologize, we're both too engrossed in the scene before us.

The center of the room is empty. The two sofas that normally sit in an L shape before our large stone fireplace are pushed to the side, along with our coffee table. A small folding table is near the far wall, laden with a small assortment of drinks, disposable cups, and a few other items I can't distinguish.

Despite all these changes to the room, the events next to the fireplace capture my attention and hold it.

My grandma wears a blindfold and is floating about three feet above the ground. In her left hand, she's holding a paper cutout that appears to be a brown stick. In between laughter, her audience is shouting.

"Left."

"No, your other left."

"Forward."

A couple more seconds of observation and I realize they're playing a variation of pin the tail on the donkey. Only this version is pin the broom under the witch.

A couple feet ahead of my grandma, a poster hangs high on the wall with several other "broom" cutouts attached at rather precarious angles. No one has even come close to the blank spot underneath the printed witch.

I move forward, taking the spot between Sylvia and Marc. "How is she floating?" I ask quietly, to no one in particular.

Marc smiles down at me as Sylvia yells, "Further left!"

He winces at her volume before answering my question. "It's a flotation potion. Good for swimming, or hovering a few feet above the ground." He ends the statement with a laugh. "One sip wears off in about five minutes or so."

I nod, unable to tear my eyes away from my grandma. She moves her arms through the air like she's swimming. As I watch, she noticeably drifts closer to the ground. Within seconds, she's standing upright on the living room carpet, visually confirming Marc's words.

"You didn't even make it to the board, Molly," my dad goads.

She huffs, yanking the blindfold off her head, then quips back, "You haven't played yet, Arthur. Let's see you do better."

My father quickly shuts his mouth as his face pales, but my grandma doesn't drop it. She approaches him, handing over the blindfold with a smug look.

My dad accepts the scrap of fabric reluctantly, and asks, "What do I get if I win?"

Tapping two fingers against her chin, my grandma contemplates. After a minute, she dips her head. "If you win, Arthur, I will buy everyone here ice cream." The crowd gathered in our living room cheers. "BUT," my grandma continues loudly over the ruckus. "If you lose, you have to buy everyone here ice cream."

My dad surveys the room as if calculating the potential cost of losing in ice cream dollars. After his eyes scan our guests, he steps forward extending his hand. "Deal."

Once the ice cream agreement has been bartered, Tricia pours a couple of drops from a vial of shimmery blue liquid into a plastic shot glass and hands it to my father. He accepts the shot glass and quickly downs the liquid, grimacing slightly as it enters his mouth.

He rises in the air almost immediately, slipping the blindfold over his eyes once he's a couple inches above the ground. I watch in fascination as his body continues to rise. First eight inches off the floor, then fourteen inches, then two feet. He drifts higher into the air until he finally stops around the three-foot mark, the same height my grandma had been when we walked in.

Sylvia's dad rushes forward and grabs my dad's shin, using the legs as leverage to spin him in two quick circles. When he finishes spinning, my dad groans lightly. He is predisposed to motion sickness and I'm surprised he's willing to play. It was probably my grandma's challenge, forcing his hand.

My dad waves his arms in the air, making a breast-stroke movement. The ridiculous motion causes me to giggle, but everyone else breaks out into loud bellowing shouts.

Sylvia's dad attempts to help my dad. "Arthur, go right!"

Meanwhile, my grandma attempts sabotage. "Left! Down! Blue!"

Despite the ridiculousness of his movements, the mid-air breaststroke proves to be quite effective. My dad reaches the wall in less than two minutes. He makes an oomph noise as he slams against the drywall, not realizing how close he was. This causes majority of the adults to laugh.

I also giggle, my eyes transfixed as my dad gropes across the wall, searching for the poster. His fingertips eventually hit the edge, and he yells, "Booyah."

My dad skims his hand over the game board until his fingertips touch the top. He adds his other hand, spreading his palms apart until one rests on each corner. The room quiets as we all watch in fascination.

His fingers move against the wall, one stopping halfway across and the other stopping three-quarters down. He slides them until they meet on the poster board... in the exact spot of the missing broom.

He pushes his cut out against the poster seconds prior to his descent. When his feet tap against the floor, my dad tears off the blindfold to check his placement. Throwing a fist into the air, he yells, "Yes!"

My mom rushes him and places a kiss against his cheek. "My hero," she exclaims dramatically. He slings his arm around her so she can't retreat, and smacks a loud kiss against her lips. When they separate, she lets out a girlish giggle.

"Your child is present," I shout dramatically.

They both ignore me. Keeping his arm around my mom, my dad twirls to face my grandma. "You owe us some ice cream!"

My grandma fakes a groan of agony, but a wide grin is spreading across her face. Her gaze locks on my mom's happy smile as she concedes defeat, "Okay, okay. Ice cream on me."

My parents haven't made an issue out of my grandma and I spending time together, but this is the first time she's been over to my parents' house. The first time we've all spent together as a family. The rift between them my grandma and mom still exists, but today it seems like that gaping hole is healing. At least a tiny bit.

16

THE RETURN

Mirabella

I naturally wake early. The sun shines through my balcony doors, bringing a bright and chipper ambience to my entire room, which infuses into my mood. I swing my legs over the edge of my bed and decide to spend the day in my studio. I've neglected my art recently and I miss it.

The second my feet hit the carpet, I remember the events of yesterday. I'm a licensed witch now!

The thought enhances my lighthearted happiness and I dance towards my closet, tripping over my feet as I pull on paint splattered overalls and a white t-shirt. My joy lightens my steps as I enter my studio.

I don't snap back to reality until my phone dings with a text. When I look at it, Sylvia's name flashes across my screen. I open her message and quickly scan her words, curious why she's awake so early. As the message registers, my tight hold on my phone loosens. I barely catch it, prior to the thin glass smashing against the floor.

Shaking my head, I read the text again: **Not 100% certain, BUT I think I just passed Vlad running down the Main Road. It was only a glimpse. Then he turned onto a dirt path and entered the woods.**

Shock and elation swirl together, flooding my system with emotion. Vlad is... back?

I rise to my feet to rush out the door and hunt for him. As I hit the hallway, I pause. Why didn't he come to my house? Or call? Or even send a text message?

I stand, frozen, wavering with indecision.

What if it isn't Vlad? Or What if he doesn't want to see me?

Inhaling a deep breath, I push aside my doubts and continue to my bedroom. I snatch up my purse and contemplate changing for half a second before discarding the idea. I hustle down the stairs and out the front door.

Standing next to my car, nerves strike again. Should I go to the Mort's? I inhale a deep, calming breath, and shake my hands to loosen up my muscles.

Vlad is back. Vlad is okay. These are both good things. On my exhale, I pull on the handle to my Prius and jump inside.

The drive to Vlad's house is normally twelve minutes, with my slow and cautious driving. Today, that twelve minutes is the equivalent of an eternity. I talk myself down from turning around at least four times.

Vlad will want to see me.

... I'm pretty sure. He probably just lost his phone, or is busy with his parents.

I work to convince myself, all the way up to the point of parking in front of his house. Turning the key to shut off my Prius, I pause for another moment. It's now or never. I chant the words on repeat as I approach the door.

Raising my hand, I make a fist and knock with three quick raps. I pause, waiting to see if I hear anyone on the other side. No one comes to answer the door and there are no sounds from inside.

I attempt another knock, then step back and look around. I notice there aren't any cars in the driveway. Which is odd. My thoughts immediately jump to the idea that Vlad is hurt. Then I remember Sylvia said he was running. Sane, injured people don't jog for fun.

The whole neighborhood looks a little empty, like everyone is out living their lives. I back off the porch and onto the sidewalk, resigned to texting Vlad or stopping back later. The second my foot hits the pavement, I hear a loud cough from behind the house.

Curious, I round the side of the Mort's home, intent on investigating and potentially knocking on the back door. The woods bordering their backyard come closer into view with each step, but nothing appears to be moving in the tree line.

I turn the corner and walk into the Mort's backyard. A loud gasp leaves my lips as my eyes land on a lightly tanned, muscular form bent in half, panting.

"Vlad?" I half-whisper, worried if I talk too loudly, he might disappear. Like a vivid dream that was never there to begin with.

Vlad straightens. His shirtless torso is gleaming with sweat, his muscles rippling as he stands to his full height. He faces me, his amber eyes meeting mine as a strand of inky black hair slips forward across his forehead.

We stand there in a silent, staring contest and everything else fades away. I couldn't tell you who moved first, but within seconds I'm wound around Vlad like I'm a monkey and he's a tree. His hands grip the back of my thighs while my legs wrap around his hips. My arms around his neck barely support any of my weight as he holds me up.

"Where have you been?" I ask, unwinding an arm from his neck to stroke a hand down his cheek.

He continues to stare deeply into my eyes without answering. Vlad inches his face closer, his eyes flitting to my lips. It's the only warning I get before his mouth latches onto mine. Vlad's tongue runs across the seam of my mouth. The motion has my lips falling open to his, and he immediately plunges his tongue inside.

Vlad devours me with teeth, tongue, and lips. Ravaging me with his kisses and pulling me closer with each swipe across my mouth.

I moan and wiggle to get closer. I don't notice Vlad's steps until my back slams against the side of the

Mort's house. The movement knocks the air out of me. I gasp from the slight pain and the heat of the house seeping into my skin through my clothes.

Pulling my head away, I try to escape from Vlad's kisses, but he's like a man possessed and chases after my lips with his. His kisses are more... aggressive than I remember. Frantic, almost.

I turn my head to the side, wanting to pause our make-out session for a conversation. Before I complete the movement, he slides one hand from beneath my thighs to cup my cheek. He uses the caress to control my skull, ensuring I can't move my face away, as I intended.

Sealing my lips tightly, I wait for Vlad to notice and pull back. He takes a second to realize I'm not responding. Vlad shifts from open-mouthed kisses to running his tongue along my lips, attempting to find a weakness.

Becoming impatient with his behavior, I open my mouth and sink my teeth into his lower lip. The bite was meant to be a warning, but I must have used more strength than I intended. The coppery tang of blood seeps into my mouth as I release my teeth from him.

Vlad releases a grunt and my weight simultaneously. My body slides down his as gravity carries me to the ground. I land heavily, stumbling a bit and placing my hands against Vlad's chest. The movement sends a whiff of a clean lemon towards me. I wrinkle my nose at the smell, wondering about the strange scent.

Before I'm able to think on it further, Vlad growls

out, "What the hell, Mira Love?" His face is furious, his tone angry and aggressive. He's holding a hand against his bleeding lip and glaring at me.

I put my hands up in a pacifying gesture. I've never seen Vlad with such an expression, and it's frightening. "I just wanted to slow down," I say, keeping my voice low and steady.

Vlad steps back, shaking his head. I use the extra space to sidestep him and move away from the house, freeing myself from the confinement he had created with his body and the wall against my back.

"I need to know what happened. Where have you been? I was so worried about you," I say calmly.

"It doesn't seem like it. Doesn't seem like you missed me at all," He mutters, pointing to his lip. His expression unchanged. He's seething.

"I'm sorry," I reply. "I didn't mean to bite that hard."

Vlad scoffs, "Sure." He steps forward menacingly. "It was just an accident," he says in a mocking tone.

His next step forward places him right in front of me. "Vlad…" I begin, but before I can finish, he shoves me with both hands, hitting me square in each shoulder.

Vlad is huge, and the strength in his push is unbelievable. I fly across the yard and smack into a tree. My head bounces off and I crumple to the ground.

I've been bullied since middle school, but I've never been afraid the actions of my tormentors would kill me. Now, however, I'm afraid I might not make it out of this situation alive.

Heaving off the ground, I pause on my hands and knees. My head is screaming in agony and I think Vlad broke a rib when he threw me across the yard. Each inhale is sharp and painful, offering no reprieve from the pain or the breathlessness flooding my body.

I'm getting lightheaded, but a glance across the yard shows Vlad heads my way. Crying out with pain, I stumble to my feet. I need to escape before he reaches me.

17

THE SAVIOR

Vlad

I wake up on cold, damp ground. Standing, I stretch all four of my legs and shake out my fur. After that, I attempt to think past a pulsing headache. It's as if my brain is pounding against my skull, blocking out everything except for a single command.

All I can think is, *run*.

Compelled by something I don't understand, I take off running. Right as my hind legs push off the ground, I raise my snout to the air and release a long howl. Three howls echo in the air in response, and the sound of twelve paws pounding on the forest floor fills my ears.

I don't register the scenery as it blurs past. The only thing that catches my eye are the flashes of brown and gold, the colors of my pack keeping pace in the trees nearby.

My instincts take over as thoughts like *danger*, *trouble*, and *run* flit across my mind with increasing intensity. I pull the dirt up with my claws as I tear through the muddy ground, hoping I'll make it in time. Needing to reach whatever my instincts are urging me towards.

It feels like days pass before I finally reach the edge of the woods. A structure is visible through the leaf-lined branches hanging down. Slowing to a stop, I crouch. My legs are shaky from the brutal pace of my run. My wolf's mind cannot accurately tell time, and I have no estimate for how long it took to arrive.

As I look ahead, the pulsing in my brain, which had quieted, intensifies. I hear three sets of paws closing in behind me. Knowing my pack will be here soon as back up, I stalk forward to assess the situation.

A few yards away, a shirtless man stands near the structure. Only the side of his face is visible. The features look familiar, but I ignore that, watching strides towards the edge of the woods. My eyes follow his intended path and land on a small form huddled on the ground, attempting to stand.

The urges I've been experiencing, warning me of danger and telling me to run, pulse through my mind with severity. Nothing else registers as I bound towards the prone figure. I near and realize it's a female human. A small, female human.

Her scent hits my nose on the next step and it's one

I recognize. With a growl, I leap over the tiny human and place myself between her and the approaching figure. My wolf instincts finally quiet. This is where I need to be.

A growl rips from my throat and my hackles rise, but the man doesn't cease his approach. The rest of my pack breaks through the trees and fans out, forming a half-circle, two on the left and one on the right.

"Vlad?" The miniscule human whispers.

Immediately after, a small hand tentatively strokes down the fur of my leg. The touch triggers something inside, and my body ripples with pain. My front legs bend and bones snap and break and rearrange. I feel my fur receding into my body and my shape changing in size and stature.

In seconds, I'm standing on the ground on two feet. The agony of my shift quickly fades and the wolf instincts that drove me to ignore my surroundings, recede. I pivot awkwardly to face the woods, stumbling slightly on my two legs instead of four.

My brain registers the damp soil, squishing beneath my toes first. Then, a hank of long, blonde hair attached to a tiny female captures my attention. "Mira?" I ask, tentatively, kneeling to inspect her.

She's on her knees with one hand planted on the ground and the other clasped against her ribs. My movements cause her to shrink backwards. I'm hurt, but I pause, waiting for her gray eyes to meet mine.

The second they do; she does a double take. Glancing at me, her eyes then flit to the lawn towards the forgotten man. "Vlad?" Mira gasps. "Why are you naked? And how are there two of you?"

"Two of me?" I repeat. Then I twirl around to stare at... me. "Who are you?" I bellow, my voice low and angry.

The imposter's eyes widen in surprise, and he stops advancing. "Why I'm Vladimir Mort. And you are...?" The words that leave the imposter's body are growly and low. He's mocking me, but unable to replicate the sound of my voice.

My gaze locks on the golden wolf from my pack, and I tilt my head in silent communication. He slinks into position, placing himself between Mira and the imposter.

With Mira protected, I stride across my parent's backyard, stopping when I'm a few steps away from the stranger. He swipes out with his leg, hoping surprise will give him the upper hand. I jump quickly into the air, relying on my wolf reflexes to help me fight against myself.

Throwing out my right hand, I jab at the imposter's throat, but he ducks and I miss. His next hit glances my rib cage and steals my breath. I don't have time to baby the minor injury. Instead, I kick out with my left leg, aiming for the imposter's knee.

By a chance of fate, my strike hits. He steps back to take weight off his injury and somehow loses his balance. Advancing forward, I grab him by the throat and push him up against the side of the house before he has a chance to recover.

Moving my second hand to his throat, I tighten my grip. I watch as his eyes bulge and he struggles more urgently for breath with both his limbs and lungs. "I'm going to put you down. But if you try anything, I will let my pack tear you apart," I warn.

My hands release the imposter's throat. He hits the ground heavily and sinks to his knees. I allow him to inhale three deep, gulping breaths before I repeat my earlier question, "I'm going to ask you one more time. Who are you?"

Still struggling for air, the imposter smirks at me from the ground. He pulls a vial of cloudy, gray-colored liquid from his short's pocket. His eyes meet mine intensely, and I step back, worried he's going to douse me in his potion.

A laugh trickles from the imposter's throat. It's an odd experience to see my double, but hear a stranger's laugh and voice. With another smirk, the imposter guzzles down the contents of the vial.

As the last drop leaves the vial, a bright light flashes. I avert my gaze to avoid it. When my eyes move back to the spot that held the imposter, a lanky, blonde-haired guy I've never seen before is now seated there.

Before I'm able to ask 'who are you?' for the third time, Mira's voice carries across the clearing. "Leif?" She asks, incredulously.

I turn and see she's standing, one hand gripped tightly around her ribs and the other grasping the fur of the golden wolf. My eyes scan her form and assess.

During the drama with the imposter, I had forgotten she appeared hurt.

She looks in pain, but not enough to require urgent medical attention. Her expression is furious as she looks around me to stare at the stranger in my backyard.

Pivoting around, I glimpse an apologetic look flash in this Leif guy's eyes, before he hurries to explain in a pleading tone. He rises to his feet with his hands clasped together. "I'm sorry, Mira. This was just a harmless prank, mostly. It got a little out of hand..."

Mira makes a scoffing noise and Leif steps to the left, trying to meet her gaze. I immediately step in front of him once more. At the same time, a chorus of growls erupts from behind me.

Leif isn't done with his pseudo-apology apparently and continues, "I thought maybe I could convince you to come with me. If you didn't—"

"You need to leave." Mira's voice is firm as she interrupts Leif's explanation. I half turn to face her and see her hard gaze.

"Mira Love." He says her name like it's a prayer. I can tell without even looking at him that this guy's in love with my girl. He starts again, "Nothing can come of this. Even if your coven knows of the shifters, they would never be okay with a marriage between the two of you. You're a legacy. I'm a legacy. We make sense. If you end up with this guy," he cuts himself off to make a harsh gesture at me. "If you end up with this guy, your children won't even be witches. His genes will be dominant. Is that what you want?"

The imposter's words hit me hard. Mira and I can't have witch children? Children aren't even a thought that's crossed my mind. We've barely even begun dating. But a family seems like something that would be important to Mira.

I watch as she takes a few strained steps forward. She grips onto the golden wolf for support, as he slowly matches each of her steps.

Resigned, I think this is it. He got her with his talk of bloodlines and legacies.

Although I only understood half of what he was talking about, I realize he can give Mira things that I can't. My shoulders slump as I watch her approach. As she nears, I step back, opening the path for her to reach Leif.

To my surprise, Mira angles her body back towards me. The second I realize her intended destination; I stride the rest of the way across the yard to meet her. She releases the golden wolf to take the last step in my direction as I approach. I gingerly wrap my arm around her waist, gently pulling her into my side.

A sigh of contentment fights to escape, but I stifle it. I want to hear what Mira needs to say. She pushes against my side, and together we face Leif.

Mira squares her shoulders, brushing against me in the process. I glance down in time to see her lift her chin haughtily, as she stares down a man over a foot taller than her.

"Leif," she begins. "I will never move to your coven with you. I'm sorry the other two times I said that didn't make it clear. But I am telling you again, for the last time. My place is here. In Florence. Please leave, I don't want to spend any more time in your presence."

The imposter deflates at her harsh words, while I internally cheer on my girl. Mira is strong and capable, and there's nothing like watching her stand up for herself.

Leif dips his head without meeting either of our eyes. "Goodbye, Mira Love. For what it's worth, I am sorry. To both of you."

He turns away and walks around the side of my parent's house. My eyes track his departure until I feel Mira sag against me.

Scooping her up into both arms, I wave away the concern of the golden wolf hovering nearby. He's been running with the pack for weeks, keeping an eye on me and the other two wolves. But before then, I honestly don't recall ever seeing him in Florence.

The wolf hesitantly gravitates towards the woods as I feel around the doorframe of my parent's house for the hide-a-key. Unlocking the door, I stride inside to situate Mira on a bed and call someone for help. As I close the door behind us, I see the golden wolf just beyond the tree line, sitting on his haunches, watching the house.

18

THE RECOVERY

Mirabella

I wake under a swath of blankets with something cool pressed against my side. Forcing my eyes to focus, I find myself in a simple room with few furnishings. My gaze slides across the surfaces and happiness settles deep into my bones when I recognize Vlad's belongings.

Inhaling deeply, the ocean and pine scent that represents Vlad teases my nostrils. He's home. The real Vlad is home. And I'm at his house.

The door to the bedroom slowly slides inward. Vlad's dark hair and broad shoulders come into view and a swarm of butterflies takes flight in my stomach. His amber gaze connects with mine and an intense sizzling connection flares between us.

"Vlad," I whisper. Seeing him now, fully clothed, brings back memories of his shift in the woods. My cheeks blush and I tip my head to the side as I remember his very muscular, very nude body.

He tosses something onto the nightstand and clambers into bed with me. Laying on his side, he gathers me up, blankets and all, gently pulling me against him. I release a hiss from the jostling motion, which causes a brief twinge in my ribs.

"Shit. Are you okay, Mira?" He asks, lifting his head to inspect me. His warm amber gaze scans down my body as if his eyes can identify exactly where I hurt through the blankets.

"I'm okay," I reassure him. "It was just a small twinge, and I'm already feeling much better than before."

A sheepish look steals over Vlad's face. "I called your grandmother and told her what happened... she brought over a vial of something saying it would heal you quicker."

I groan. "How long have I been out?"

"A few hours..." Vlad replies, leaving it as an open-ended statement.

Sighing, I ask, "How many of them are out there?"

Vlad laughs. "Your parents, my parents, your grandmother, Sylvia, and Marc."

"And Marc?" I question, surprised he rushed over at news of my injuries. Then again, maybe I shouldn't be. Marc always comes through with advice and assistance. Whenever I need it, even if unasked.

"Yeah. I'm not sure how he knew," Vlad replies.

I release another heartfelt sigh, "Well, we should go

out there and get it over with." Instead of immediately replying, Vlad hesitates. "What's wrong?" I ask, concerned.

He leans in, his forehead touching mine and our gazes locking intimately. Heat blazes in his eyes as our stare continues. "Would it be okay if I kissed you?" He asks. Our faces are so close, his lips graze mine as he speaks.

I tip my face up, closing the distance to press my mouth gently against his. The movement was the invitation he was waiting for. Vlad's hands snake up my body to capture my cheek and neck. He uses the leverage to move my head and control the kiss.

Unlike Leif-pretending-to-be-Vlad, Vlad doesn't pressure me to take the kiss further. His mouth caresses mine gently, then he places a kiss on each of my cheeks, his lips finally landing on my forehead. We stay that way for a few beats, his warm mouth pressed against my smooth skin.

He returns to my lips, and they fall open of their own volition. Vlad sweeps his tongue across the inside of my mouth in a deep, claiming kiss. He explores with his tongue and teeth. I moan into him, arching against his chest as I seek to get infinitesimally closer. My noises cause his muscular arms to tighten around me, as if he wants the same.

We pull apart, and Vlad rests his forehead against mine again. Both of our chests rise and fall deeply, our eyes communicating our unspoken feelings.

With a reluctant look, Vlad pulls away.

"Vlad," I start softly, not wanting to ruin our reunion, but needing answers all the same.

He exhales deeply, then nods. "I know what you're going to ask... and we have a lot to talk about." He pauses and sighs. "But I think we should see your family first. Everyone is pretty worried about you."

"Okay," I nod.

As much as I want answers, Vlad's right. We need to reassure my family that I'm okay before we can talk over everything that's happened in our time apart. "Just promise me we can talk after my family leaves."

"I promise," Vlad swears. He runs his nose up the side of my neck and inhales deeply. Then he releases his hold and climbs off the bed.

As I follow him towards the door, I grimace imagining my mom's reaction. Staying inside Vlad's bedroom can only delay it for so long, though. Sighing, I grumble, "Let's get this over with."

THREE HOURS and at least one-hundred and fifty reassurances later, my mom finally accepts that I'm okay. The Morts walk my parents out to their car, with reassurances they'll be home in case I need anything at all.

Sylvia lingers in the entryway, her assessing gaze scanning over me for the fiftieth time. "Call me tomorrow, okay?"

"Promise," I reply.

She nods and walks down the sidewalk. I give one

last wave as she peels away from the curb. Tricia and Mr. Mort return to the house as Sylvia's car rounds the corner out of sight. I close the door, then face the small group left inside.

"I'm going to start dinner," Tricia announces. She hugs me one more time, giving another one of her signature tight squeezes, then whisks away in a wave of dark hair and sweet perfume.

Her departure leaves Bart, Marc, Vlad, and I standing in an awkward cluster in the living room. Mr. Mort's eyes connect with mine a half-second before Tricia calls out from the kitchen, "Bart, can you come help me?"

"Of course, dear." He replies in his deep voice. His gaze slides across the three of us before he dips his head and follows Tricia's path into the kitchen.

"Sooo," Marc says, elongating the word as he rocks back onto his heels.

"Why are you still here?" Vlad asks, none too kindly.

"I want to know what happened... I've been worried about you. And about Mira." Marc replies, ignoring Vlad's vicious tone. "I might be able to help. That's all I want."

Vlad's lip curls. I step forward, placing my hand against his chest, hoping to stop any potential arguments. Before I became an intern at the Daily, Vlad and Marc seemed to get along. I don't want to cause tension between them, but I'm not sure how to resolve the conflicts that start whenever we're together.

"It's okay, Vlad," I say calmly. "Marc's family has a lot of knowledge of witching history. I think we should tell him everything that happened. He might be able to shed light on anything we don't understand."

When Vlad remains tense with a hard look in his eyes, I add, "He also knows about the shifters. I really think he can help."

The tension leaves Vlad's shoulders, and he nods. "Alright. But nothing leaves this room."

Vlad wraps his arm around my shoulders and guides me to the couch without waiting for Marc to agree. He sits down and pulls me onto his lap.

Marc eyes the two of us speculatively before perching on the far end of the couch. He angles his body so his legs point in our direction. "Where did you go?" He asks, sounding curious.

I wriggle, trying to leave Vlad's lap, feeling uncomfortable with the PDA in front of our boss and friend. Vlad places his large hands against my waist, holding me down firmly. I attempt to move my hips, but they no longer budge.

Resigned, I turn my upper half so both Marc and Vlad are visible. I'm equally curious to learn Vlad's whereabouts over the past few weeks.

He exhales deeply, his breath stirring the hairs on the nape of my neck and causing me to shiver. I hear his smirk in his words. "A few weeks ago, when we were at Mira's grandma's house, we ran into a small pack of wolves. One of which was the golden wolf

Mira, and I had met when we were summoned to the shifter council." He pauses, looking contemplative.

I prod him in the chest, urging him to continue. I already know this part and want to hear the rest. Before I can pull my finger away, Vlad snatches it and uses the leverage to intertwine his hand with mine.

He offers a wolfish grin, then continues, "I don't recall exactly what happened afterwards. One second, I was standing with Mira as a human, and the next I was leaping off the porch into a shift. When I hit the ground, it was with four paws."

"Where did you go? Did the wolves take you somewhere?" Marc interjects eagerly.

Vlad nods. "When we're in wolf form, we telepathically communicate with words and images. It's not the same as being a human where full sentences are used." He directs these words to me, so I can follow the next portion of his story. "The pack I was running with spoke of a spring. They said it was important... We were hoping it was the cure to the curse."

I interrupt Vlad, "Leif told me about a spring... he said a witch's jealousy over a shifter-owned spring was the origin of the curse."

Vlad's neutral expression morphs into a furious frown. "Are you referring to that fucker that was pretending to be me?" He bellows.

"Shhh," I respond urgently. The last thing I want is for Vlad's parents to come running, thinking we're under attack or something. "Calm down. Yes, Leif is that guy from earlier."

"I don't think we should trust anything from that asshole. Or did you forget that he pretended to be your boyfriend so he could kiss you, then beat you up?"

Marc's sharp inhale interrupts Vlad's tirade. Apparently, Vlad failed to disclose the details about the cause of my injuries. I ignore Marc for now and refocus on convincing Vlad that Leif's words may be true.

"Look, I'm arguably more upset about Leif's actions than you are. But he is an extremely knowledgeable witch. What he did was wrong, and I don't fully understand his intentions, but that doesn't negate the fact that he knows a lot," I defend. "Plus, it sounds like the spring is real, according to your wolves, which is an awfully big coincidence. Doesn't that count for something?"

"Did you look for this spring already? Did you find it?" Marc adds.

"We ran for weeks, combing the woods up north, searching, but we couldn't locate it. The other wolves I was running with... they're stuck. They have been for a while. We were trying to find it for our own use as much as anyone else."

"What if we attempted to find it as humans?" Marc asks, excitedly. "It could be related to the cure."

I nod along with Marc's words. "Do you have any idea where it is, or what it's nearby? If you do, we could look up springs in that area to find it!"

Dragging his hands across his face, Vlad adopts a pensive expression. "It's in Canada, I know that much for sure. We crossed the border a few days after my initial shift..." He trails off. The living room is silent as Marc and I hang on to Vlad's every word. "It wouldn't be on any maps. If shifters had a secret spring, they wouldn't put it into Foogle."

"There's no way we could find it then?" I ask, defeated.

Vlad furrows his brow, his handsome features scrunched as he considers our options. "I could shift back and find the pack. If I ask them to describe the landmarks again, then those might help us pinpoint a location on a map."

His words cause a spike of anxiety. I'm not ready for Vlad to shift again. Not yet. What if he takes off like before? Then we're back to square one.

My face must reflect my trepidation. Vlad squeezes my hand and whispers, "I'll be okay, Little Mir. I've shifted dozens of times and I've always been able to change back. It was just a fluke."

I nod while Marc asks, "When can you meet with the pack?"

Vlad precedes his answer with another hand squeeze. "I think I should go now. They're probably nearby still. I don't want them to wander further into the woods before I have a chance to talk with them."

19

THE INTEL

Mirabella

Marc and I stand in the Mort's backyard, watching Vlad walk into the tree line. He's clad in only a pair of gym shorts, despite the chilly evening air. Marc was prepared for the weather, with a fleece coat in his car. Before we came outside, Vlad snagged a throw blanket for me. It's wrapped around my shoulders like a shawl, to keep warm while I wait. Even with the extra layer, I'm still chilled to the bone and I don't know how Vlad isn't freezing.

A gasp forces itself past my lips when he pulls down his shorts, his tanned skin glinting in the porch light. It's visible for mere seconds before he bends over and begins to morph and grow, changing from a human man to a fur-covered wolf. Once his shift is complete, Vlad raises his snout in the air and releases a howl.

I hold my breath until his pack answers. They're still here.

Together, Marc and I watch Vlad run into the forest. Once he's out of sight, I sense Marc's attention shift to me. I ignore his steady gaze, my eyes fixated on the woods.

His words barely register as I eye the trees with bated breath. "Mira, what happened with Leif?" His tone is concerned and cautious, like he's nervous about my response.

I drag my eyes away from the woods to meet Marc's emerald gaze. "He took some potion... it made him look like Vlad. Then he planted himself so he would be seen and waited behind Vlad's house..." I trail off, vividly recalling the events from earlier. I'm disappointed by Leif and hurt by his actions.

"Then what?" Marc asks. I can tell he's forcing himself to remain calm while listening.

"He kissed me. When I tried to fight him off, he flung me across the yard into a tree."

Marc growls in his throat. I raise an eyebrow in his direction, but the sudden sound of a howl nearby has me whipping my head back towards the woods. Shortly after the noise, Vlad's wolf reappears at the tree line.

I watch, wide-eyed, as he shifts once more. He slips into his gym shorts before jogging back to us. When he reaches the back of the house, he slings an arm around my shoulders and it feels like the most natural motion in the world.

"Well?" Marc prods.

"I think I have some good intel. We can look it up in the morning and go from there," Vlad replies.

He moves his gaze from Marc, his amber eyes scanning my face to ensure I'm okay. Whatever he sees must reassure him, as he pulls us forward, through the back door and into the house.

Marc follows behind us silently as we walk towards the front door. When we reach the small entryway, our group pauses.

"Do you need a ride home, Mira?" Marc asks.

I glance to Vlad. He raises a single brow, as if he's also waiting for my response.

Locking onto his amber gaze, I reply, "I think I'm going to stay here." Vlad nods his approval and I tear my eyes away to address Marc, "I'll text you in the morning after we have more information."

"I need to go with you to the spring... I want to know what's happening." Marc murmurs softly, while staring deeply into my eyes. Despite the low volume of his words, they sound urgent.

I start to wonder why Marc is so invested, then remind myself that his family has expansive records of witching history. He probably wants to know what's happening so he can continue his legacy of recording important events. I open my mouth to respond.

Vlad chooses that moment to interject, "You can

come with us. I'll research the markers they told me about—early tomorrow morning. We'll either leave after that or wait until the next day, depending on how far it is and what travel arrangements we need to make."

Marc gives a curt nod, then opens the door to let himself out without another word.

Once it closes firmly behind him, Vlad turns the lock and leads me back to his room. In a semi-familiar ritual, he grabs clothes for me and we both get ready for sleep. Within a few minutes, we slide under the covers together.

Vlad is laying on his back, staring at the ceiling. I turn towards him, propping my head on my elbow so I can watch him. He mimics my pose so we're both laying on our sides facing one another.

"I'm really kind of mad at you," I tell him, but my words lack venom.

"I would have been here if I could. There weren't many...human thoughts running through my mind. I spent most of my weeks following my survival instincts, leading the pack, and trying to find the spring. But I will tell you, I thought of you and I missed you. It's one of the few human emotions that bled through during that time." Vlad's tone is solemn, his expression serious.

I flick out my free hand and playfully whack him across the chest. "Just never do that to me again," I say to punctuate the light hit.

I don't want to hurt Vlad—well, not much—I just

want him to know that his absence caused me pain. I wasn't sure that he was ever going to come back.

"If I can prevent it, I will never leave you when you need me." His voice rumbles back.

I nod once and scoot in until I'm close enough to tuck my head underneath his propped-up chin. I wrap my arm around his waist and respond into his chest, "Thank you." Then I whisper, knowing he'll be able to hear, "And I missed you too."

Vlad nuzzles his face into my hair and slides an arm around my body to tug me closer. His firm grip molds the front of our bodies together. Within seconds, his heat and the safety of his arms lulls me to sleep.

20

THE ROADTRIP

Mirabella

Vlad drives me home to pack some clothes for our trip. He pulls up my steep driveway, parking near the top, and moves to unbuckle. I stop him with a hand on his arm. "Can you wait out here? I want to tell my parent's our plans, and I think they would react better if I went in alone."

Vlad eyes me curiously, but nods.

I'm not surprised he doesn't exactly buy my excuse, but I'm glad he isn't fighting me. I promised Sylvia that I would call her yesterday, and I want to talk without Vlad eavesdropping.

Smiling, I hop out the car and rush to the door before he can change his mind. I cross the threshold and yell, "Hello!"

No one answers or comes to the entryway. I slide my phone from my pocket and type up a quick message to my parents, so I don't forget: **Vlad and I are going camping. We will be back in a few days.**

My mom's reply pings back almost immediately: **Camping? Have fun and tell Vlad we think he should have planned something more romantic than being bitten by bugs and eating dehydrated food!** The words are accompanied by a half a dozen emojis, including a wink and a tent.

I'm not sure what my mom is encouraging, but she doesn't always use emojis correctly. Last week, she sent me several eggplant emojis accompanied with a message that said: **Guess what I'm doing today.**

When I replied: **I'm not sure I want to know...** she became a little huffy.

Her next message had a little sass as she replied: **I work so hard on growing my vegetables. I wish you and your father would at least act a little interested.**

That's when I realized she was using the eggplant emoji as a vegetable... to signify her gardening in the backyard.

Ignoring her message, I click Sylvia's name as I jog up the stairs to my room. She answers on the first ring, "Are you okay? Vlad told me what happened... I can't believe Leif did that!"

I push my bedroom door closed behind me before I respond, "Yeah, I'm okay."

Sighing, I try to organize my thoughts. I'm still not over what happened with Leif. However, if I suddenly become emotional, I know it will do more harm than good to everyone involved.

Vlad is still beating himself up over what happened, and we both know that there was nothing either of us could have done differently. Right now, there are bigger issues at play than Leif's psychotic actions.

"Honestly, I'm really disappointed in Leif." I finally say. "What he did was pretty messed up."

Sylvia laughs humorlessly. "I'd say that's the understatement of the year."

"I still can't believe it." I sigh again. "I have so many thoughts jumbling around about Leif, I'm not sure how I feel. I'm a little disappointed in myself for trusting him, but he also did so much to help me with studying. I guess I knew he wasn't exactly a saint after what happened with Kaylee. Then again, his messed-up way of defending me helped get her off my back. Afterwards, he kind of redeemed himself too, by showing he had another side."

I pause, but Sylvia waits me out, knowing I have more to say. "He also invited me to join his coven." Sylvia gasps dramatically. "I declined, of course." I add on quickly. I don't disclose that I briefly played with the idea.

Sylvia stays silent. We've been friends for years and she knows I haven't gotten to my point. My true feelings about the situation with Leif. "I just feel like he tricked me." My voice sounds defeated, even to my own ears. "I thought he was someone decent and trustworthy, then he turned out to be a total ass." I don't normally cuss, but there's no other word to describe Leif's behavior.

Sylvia hmms into the phone.

This time, I let the silence sit while she thinks about the Leif situation. While I wait, I rummage through my closet until I find a duffle bag. Then I slowly pick through my clothes and deposit the things I think I will need for camping. I've never actually been camping before, or to Canada, so I have to guess what to bring.

Once my duffle is full, I tug on the zipper to close the bag. I stop immediately when Sylvia says, "I don't think any one person is all good or all bad. Every person is a gray area. Like sometimes people are mostly good, but make an occasional bad decision. Or maybe a person is mostly bad and makes an occasional good decision. It could change any day or time. A mostly good person could decide that they're over being good and turn into a mostly bad person."

"Okaay," I reply. "Do you think Leif was a mostly bad person then?"

"No, Mira." Sylvia says, surprising me. "I think the reason you trusted Leif was because his intentions were primarily good. But some people make mistakes when they feel strongly about something. What Leif did was fucked up, but I think he did it to get you to move. Which wasn't nefarious."

I plop down on my bed, mulling over her words. "Are you saying I shouldn't be upset?"

"No," Sylvia responds firmly. "I'm saying there's no

way you could have known that Leif would act that way and you shouldn't beat yourself up for trusting him. He was trustworthy. He just made a shitty decision."

"Do you think I should forgive him?" I ask, curious to hear her response.

"I think you need to give it time and see how you feel then."

We hang up our call and I drift back downstairs, lost in thought. When I near Vlad's sports car idling in the driveway, he rolls down the window and asks, "Have everything you need?"

"I think so," I reply, holding up the small black duffle.

Vlad jumps out and meets me halfway. He grabs my bag, then walks to my side of the car and opens the door. I watch in the side mirror as he pops the trunk and stows my duffle with some camping supplies he brought from his house.

"Ready to go meet Marc?" He asks as he reverses down the driveway.

Determinedly, I push all thoughts of Leif to the back of my mind. After my talk with Sylvia, I'm not sure how I feel, but for right now there are bigger things to focus on.

"Let's pick up Marc and find the spring."

Marc rented a massive SUV and crammed it full of more camping gear than an outdoor supply store. At first, I thought the pure size of the vehicle, and volume of snacks, were excessive. However, after seven hours on the road, I've become appreciative of his forethought.

I'm lounging in the second row crunching through a bag of chips while Marc and Vlad sit in the front arguing over directions. The scenery passes in a steady blur, quickly distracting me from the boys. I wish I brought art supplies.

Marc's voice surprises me from my thoughts. "It's starting to get late. We should stop at the next town and find a place to stay for the night. I don't want any of us to drive while tired. While we're there, we can check and see if they have a store with a sketchpad and some colored pencils or something for you, Mira."

My initial surprise over his statement transitions to gratitude as emerald eyes connect with mine through the rearview mirror. I flash a smile of gratitude, which Marc returns eagerly.

"She prefers paint,' Vlad interjects.

I laugh. "I prefer paint, but pencils or even charcoal would be okay for the car."

"We'll try to find you something," Marc confirms.

When no one continues the conversation, Marc fiddles with the radio until some old rock softly fills the silence. My eyes return to my window, mentally snapshotting the picturesque mountains. It doesn't take long for a sign indicating the next town to appear.

"Hope, BC," Vlad reads.

"Seems like a fitting place to stop on this trip,"

Marc says. Although his words are light, his tone reflects the somber situation.

He turns, taking the exit towards Hope. Soon the trees give way to suburban houses evenly spaced and nestled safely between picket fences. We continue to drive, eventually entering a downtown area. I move my face closer to the window to inspect the store fronts.

Downtown Hope appears similar to Florence. Stout buildings made of brick line the streets. As we drive, I see families enjoying ice cream and couples walking in and out of shops. I haven't traveled very far from home, and I'm fascinated by the small city. It makes me wonder if every small town is the same or if Hope is just weirdly similar to Florence.

We approach the end of the connected buildings and turn into a parking lot advertising a motel. The sun is setting on the dusky town as Marc pulls the massive SUV into a parking spot.

We all clamber out, groaning and stretching. I'm thankful for the reprieve after a long day of sitting. The guys head towards the motel entrance to obtain rooms for the night, but I linger near the edge of the lot.

After a few steps, Vlad realizes I'm not following him and glances back at me. I glance between him and downtown. Then I shout, "While you two book rooms at the hotel, I'm going to walk down the street. I think I saw an art store."

Vlad nods hesitantly. He doesn't immediately move to join Marc, and I internally debate extending an invite for him to join me. Just as I open my mouth, Vlad says, "Just be safe, okay?"

"I will. I have my phone."

Vlad nods again. Then he jogs towards the motel lobby to catch up with Marc.

I watch him for a second longer before exiting the parking lot onto the main road. My eyes scan my surroundings as I walk down the sidewalk. The entire time my fingers itch to sketch the trees and the mountains.

In the setting sun, I attempt to backtrack the roads we traveled to the motel and find the art store. Three wrong turns later and I'm feeling defeated. Inhaling deeply, I take one more turn before giving up.

As I round the corner, I spot a store labeled "The Art Shop". I check the hours posted near the door and the shop is open for about a half hour longer. With no time to lose, I pull open the door. A small bell jingles, announcing my presence as I wander inside.

21

THE ROOM

Mirabella

I return to the motel laden down with three bags of art supplies. Surprisingly, the store was very well stocked. They even had a few things I plan to bring home with me for my studio.

Entering the lobby, I smile towards the receptionist, but she isn't paying any attention to me. She's focusing on a magazine placed on the countertop.

I heave my bags of new supplies onto a floral arm chair and drag my phone out of my back pocket. I need to Vlad for our room numbers. When my screen lights up, I see texts from both him and Marc already waiting.

Vlad's just has a number: **203.**

I'm assuming this is our room, but click on Marc's text to confirm: **Vlad said you two were okay to share** a room. You're in 203 and I'm in 204. Let me know when you're back safe.

I type a quick message to Marc: **Back! See you in the morning.**

Then, I grab the handles to my bags and exit the lobby. From there, I approach the stairs leading to the second floor and clamber up.

The motel is one of those two story buildings with the lobby off to one side. The stairs are on the other, leading up to one long balcony. The entries to each room are attached to the exterior of the building.

Following the signs, I direct myself to room 203. I reach the door and fumble with my bags, trying to free a hand to knock. Before I'm able to transfer everything to one side, the door opens, and a slightly rumpled, shirtless Vlad leans against the doorframe.

"Hey," he rumbles in a deep voice. Leaning forward, he slides his fingers past mine, into the handles of the bags.

I smile gratefully as I slip my fingers out, leaving him to carry them in. He turns sideways and I slide through the small space left between him and the door.

Glancing around, I inspect the room. A large bed sits in the center with the white bedding already hosting a Vlad shaped imprint. Across from the bed is a dark, wooden dresser with a large TV on top. Next to the TV, there's a small circular table with four chairs. Visible further down the room are two closed doors, which I assume are the bathroom and closet. The room is modest, but clean. And it's definitely better than the car.

When the door closes, a luggage rack holding both our duffle bags becomes visible. "Thanks for bringing my bag up," I murmur.

Vlad nods, striding past to place my art supplies on the table. "You're welcome," he says, as he ambles back to the bed, settling himself into the rumpled spot.

I tear my gaze away from his chiseled upper body to unzip my duffel and retrieve my pajamas. I walk towards the doors at the back of the room, looking for the bathroom.

"Door on the right," Vlad's voice rumbles, sounding half-asleep already.

Following his instructions, I open the door to the right to reveal a simple bathroom. I quickly change into my pajamas, brush my teeth, and splash some water on my face.

By the time I re-enter the main room, Vlad has already fallen into a deep sleep. His eyes are closed and his chest rises and falls with each deep breath.

I lean against one of the walls, briefly observing Vlad's peaceful slumber. His normally intense, chiseled face is relaxed. His plush lips are slightly parted and his strong brow is flattened with a chunk of his inky black hair hanging over it.

My eyes skim down his body, noting his broad shoulders, toned abs, and lean waist. The longer I stare, the more my skin heats. Like I suddenly have a fever. I force myself to turn away and find something less creepy to do.

Despite our early start, I'm still brimming with energy. I contemplate climbing into bed and hoping for sleep, but ultimately decide to break in some of my new art supplies, instead. Padding quietly to the table, I silently slip my new notepad and pencil set out of my bags. Careful not to crinkle the thick plastic, I carry them around to the far side of the table and settle into the chair. My hand grabs a color at random and flies across the page.

Soon I'm totally engrossed in my art, blending and coloring until an image starts to take shape on the page.

A small movement catches the corner of my eye and I glance up as Vlad rolls to his side. His hand searches across the bed for a moment, making me think he's woken up, until he snores and stills again.

My heart melts a little at the thought of Vlad searching for me. Vlad is so forceful when he's awake and so handsome. Sometimes I'm not quite sure what he sees in me, but Vlad treats me like I'm special. And I enjoy it.

I return to my notepad and continue dragging pencils across the paper. My eyes grow tired, but I forge ahead until the image finally feels complete. With a few final swipes of color, I know that it's finished.

I prop up my notepad, then scoot my chair back to assess what I've created. The vivid blues and greens immediately draw my eyes in, forcing me to examine the details first. My gaze finally focuses on the entire image and I gasp.

Snatching the notepad, I rip off the page and rush into the bathroom. I shred the paper into pieces, then those pieces into smaller pieces. Over and over, I repeat the process until I'm left with only the tiniest scraps of paper. Standing over the toilet, I let each piece drift into the basin until they're all soaked with water. I push down the handle and watch them swirl away.

I step back and sag against the countertop. The heat I felt earlier has left my body completely. I feel cold and drained. Sickly. Inhaling a few deep breaths, I attempt to calm my racing heart and collect myself before exiting. After a few minutes, my heartbeat slows and I'm no longer on the verge of a panic attack.

Opening the door as quietly as I can, I tiptoe into the room. The fear flowing through my veins has washed away all of my tiredness, but I need the comfort that Vlad can offer. When the bed comes into view, I discover Vlad sitting upright, his face etched with concern.

"Mira, is everything okay?" He asks, his voice groggy with sleep.

"I'm not sure," I respond.

Vlad pats the bed next to him twice, and that's the only invitation I need. I slip under the covers next to him. Vlad clicks off the lamp, eliminating the soft glow and steeping us in darkness. He gathers me in his arms and tugs me against his hard, warm body. As his warmth and strength envelope me, my previous tension drains away.

A soft kiss hits the hair above my ear a second before Vlad whispers, "Goodnight, Little Mir."

He instantly falls asleep, but I whisper into the silent room anyway, "Thank you, Vladimir Mort."

I WAKE EARLY the next morning feeling well rested and warm. Slowly, I force my sleep crusted eyes to open. They immediately focus on an amber gaze hovering inches above my face.

The second we lock eyes, Vlad swoops down and seals his lips to mine in a claiming kiss. I moan as he glides his tongue through my mouth, giving a quick nip to my lower lip, then retreating. Before I'm able to protest his departure, he runs his nose down the side of my neck.

I feel his deep inhale first, then the scrape of stubble as he retraces the path with his mouth. He peppers light, suctioning kisses down the side of my neck until he reaches the collar of my shirt.

A questioning gaze meets mine as Vlad plays with the lower hem. Without giving it too much thought, I whisper my consent to his unspoken question, "Yes."

The word barely passes through my lips before he's tugging the shirt up and over my head. Vlad throws my top behind him, into the room, then sits back on his haunches. His gaze rakes over my naked upper half, stopping to fixate on my breasts. My nipples harden under his hungry gaze. I fight the urge to cover myself, forcing my hands to flatten on the bed. This is the first time I've ever been half-naked with someone.

Vlad leans forward and suctions his mouth to my left nipple and any thoughts of covering up immediately flee. He laves his tongue over the sensitive bud, while using his left hand to knead the delicate skin of my right breast. I moan, enjoying the sensations Vlad evokes with just a few touches.

He switches his mouth and hand, alternating his attention to each breast. When he finally lifts his head, I'm panting with desire, arched off the bed for easy access. Vlad's eyes connect with mine, smoldering.

Our mouths connect once more and he devours me with his kisses. My hardened nipples brush his bare chest, heightening my desire. Vlad's fingers slowly drift down my stomach, pausing to play with the top of my shorts. My butt lifts of its own accord and his hardness brushes against my hip. He slides the shorts down my body slowly, waiting until the last second to break our kiss.

He eyes my body hungrily, peppering a few light kisses across my belly and upper thighs. He returns to the top of the bed, laying a hand across my lower abdomen, his amber gaze meeting mine. Heat sizzles where our skin connects.

"I want to touch you, is that okay?" He asks.

I don't have to think about my reply. My center is

soaked and throbbing, my nipples hard and achy. "Yes, don't stop."

Vlad immediately resumes kissing me greedily while he shoves my panties down. His thick fingers delve into my folds. Vlad pushes slightly inside, whispering sweet words against my lips as he does. He uses my own wetness to slick his fingers through my folds and across my nub. Striking the same spot over and over until I'm clinging to his neck with a whimper.

His mouth leaves mine to suck on my nipple once more. The first tug on the sensitive bud has my entire body tensing. I feel like I'm on the precipice of a cliff and the next stroke of Vlad's fingers has me falling off the edge into intense pleasure. I moan out his name as he extends the pulses with a few well-timed strokes.

Vlad removes his hand and moves his body to hover above me. He fits his lower half against mine. His erection strains against the gym shorts he wore to sleep, creating a light friction against my still sensitive skin.

I give him a sly look, then run my hands down his chest and the ridges of his abs until my fingers meet the waistband of his shorts. Keeping our gazes connected, I play with the hem, mimicking his motions from earlier.

Vlad's voice is raspy and desperate as he mutters, "Please."

Feeling powerful, I slip my hands under the band. They slide over his deep V, stopping to tightly grasp his erection. A wave of nerves tries to wash over me, but I shove them away. I grip onto his hardened length with one hand, sliding up and down the silken skin firmly.

Vlad groans and resumes kissing me. He thrusts his hips in time with my strokes, matching the movements with his tongue in my mouth. I use my free hand to slide down his shorts, freeing his cock firmly gripped in my hand. Still exploring, I tentatively grip one of his tight balls in my hand. I give it a light squeeze and Vlad groans against my lips. His reactions make me bold and I push on him to roll to his side.

We lie facing each other and both watch my hand as it strokes up and down. His penis is much larger than anticipated, thick and long. My hand can only cover a portion of it.

A knock sounds at our door, and I startle. I stop my movements and loosen my grip, turning my head as if I can see through the wood.

Vlad quickly recaptures my attention, firmly gripping my cheek and meeting my lips with a hard kiss. He nips and licks while his erection resumes thrusting into my hand. I tighten my squeeze and return his kisses eagerly.

The person at the door becomes persistent, banging with a fist louder than before. I tear my lips away from Vlad's just as a muffled voice calls, "It's Marc. We need to get going soon, if we want to make it there before dark."

Vlad groans. He kisses my lips gently, then carefully removes my fingers and pulls up his shorts. He strides to the door and opens it a sliver, partially hiding as he addresses Marc. "We'll get ready now. I need to take a shower first and Mira isn't awake yet," he lies.

Marc's voice is barely audible as he responds, and I can't make out his words.

Vlad replies, "Okay, we'll text you." Then he shuts the door without waiting for a response.

Vlad strides back to the bed like a man on a mission. He lifts me bridal style and carries me towards the bathroom.

"Where are we going?" I ask, my voice sounding unrecognizably breathy.

"To get cleaned up," he replies with a wolfish grin.

22

THE SPRING

Mirabella

Marc pulls the SUV into a large dirt circle, angling the vehicle to park. He doesn't make it into the imaginary lines he's drawn in the "lot", so he backs up and straightens out before shutting the vehicle off.

"Is it near here?" I ask, surveying our surroundings.

After sixteen hours in the car over two days, this place doesn't look like anything special. To the left is the dirt road we drove in on. Winding its way down the mountain through the trees and tall grass to a small town and a larger highway. To the right is a steep mountainside, peppered with more trees. There's a dirt path near a weathered wooden sign that I'm guessing is a trailhead.

"This is it," Marc confirms.

Vlad is also surveying the area from the passenger

seat and I wonder if he's equally unimpressed. He finishes and interjects, "It's pretty late. We need to set up camp for the night." He turns to Marc. "Should we hike in on the trail and set up, or just make a camp here in the parking lot for tonight?"

Marc scans the area, then glances at me in the rearview mirror. I quirk a brow and his lips tug up on one corner. After the exchange, his gaze shifts to Vlad. "How far out is the spring?"

Vlad's reply comes quickly, "Just over three miles."

"I think we set up here for the night. If we leave early enough, we'll be able to hike three miles, check the spring and hike back in one day. Especially since it stays light out later here. We can bring gear, but it will lighten our packs quite a bit if we don't bring everything with us. Does that work for both of you?" Marc asks, making eye contact with both Vlad and I.

Vlad and I exchange a glance, then return our gaze to Marc. As a unit, we exit the SUV. Marc directs us, requesting various items from the trunk, arranging them at the edge of the trees. Between the three of us, it's quick work.

Once everything is situated, I sit on a cooler and watch Vlad and Marc wrangle a giant tent into existence. The result is a beige and green monstrosity large enough for at least twelve people. I unzip the canvas and step inside to check it out, half expecting the fabric to be magic and contain separate rooms and beds. Unfortunately, it's just a regular tent and all that's inside is more canvas.

With a sigh, I return to the dirt outside and find the guys filling air mattresses. The loud whir of the electric pump makes it impossible to converse. I linger near the canvas flap, watching until they finish.

Once the air mattresses are situated inside, Marc asks, "Can you set up the sleeping bags?"

"Of course," I reply.

I jump off the cooler and scan the dirt until I find a stack of rolled sleeping bags outside the tent. I take my time unrolling each one and arranging it just so before moving to the next. I throw the covers in the corner, then exit the tent once more.

It's darker outside, and Marc is building a fire. He already has a small blaze that is gradually building higher with each stick he adds. I pick up a few twigs between the tent and the fire, for extra fuel that I'm sure we'll need later.

Marc nods his approval. "Thanks Mira, I haven't collected firewood yet."

Wanting to help, I wander closer to the edge of the forest to find bigger chunks of wood. Vlad's voice stops my steps prior to passing the first tree. "Don't go into the woods. We don't know what's out there... it might not be safe."

Nodding, I return to the fire with my measly pile of twigs and toss them on the ground near Marc. With nothing else to do, I plop into a folding chair. The boys join me, perching on chairs on either side of me. Marc prepares a bean concoction in a pot.

We eat in companionable silence as the sun sets,

and the fire creates long shadows in the dark. "Are the wolves going to join us here?" I ask Vlad.

He opens his mouth to reply, but a long howl cuts through the air, interrupting him. "Sounds like they're already here," he replies with a grin.

I smile at the expression of joy reflected in Vlad's eyes. It's clear the pack has become very important to him and he's happy to have them with us.

Our eyes remain connected. The smile drops off Vlad's face and his expression transitions to a devious smirk. His amber eyes convey a sizzling heat. My body fills with tension and I fight the urge to launch myself towards him.

"Let's finish our dinner and clean up. We have a long day ahead of us tomorrow," Marc states dryly, interrupting our stare down.

My cheeks flush with heat, and I tear my eyes away from Vlad. I scarf down my meal and rinse my bowl with water, studiously avoiding the gaze of both boys as I return to the tent.

BY THE TIME we finally stop for a break, my feet are sore. I regret not investing in a pair of hiking boots for our trip. Or exercising more to prepare. Overall, I am not in any shape to hike six miles seeking a spring that could solve a centuries old curse affecting witches and shifters.

"Is it much further?" I ask, plopping myself down onto a log, then stretching my achy muscles out.

We've been walking for almost three hours, but the time isn't even the worst part. The trail has carried us up a steep incline, only to wind downhill a half hour later. Then repeat the pattern. Over and over. Up, then down, then up and down again.

The guys haven't complained a single time, despite carrying packs of gear. Even now, Marc shrugs wordlessly, gently perching next to me and pulling my leg across his lap to massage my muscles.

Vlad sits on my other side, removing a map from the side pouch of his backpack. Cell service out here is non existent, but luckily Marc prepared. Vlad turns the paper this way and that with a furrowed brow. "We're close. I think our destination is through that patch of trees over there, actually." He motions to a large batch of fir trees that look the same as all the other fir trees. "The spring should be just a few meters past there."

Excitedly, I leap off the log. Ignoring the pangs of protest from my tender feet. I march to the patch of trees. As we work our way through the thick foliage, a large clearing becomes visible.

My hands are suddenly clammy from nerves. Whatever we find past these trees has the potential to directly impact our lives.

It may lift the curse.

It could be the Cure.

I let my imagination run wild, as we plod across the damp earth, picking our way through the trees. I'm so lost in thought, I don't notice Vlad ahead of me, standing stock still. Instead, I run into him, bouncing half a foot backwards upon the impact to his pack. Marc is close behind and steadies me by placing his hands on my hips.

"What's wron—" I begin, stopping short when Vlad steps aside.

We're at the edge of the trees. Ahead is a large, grassy clearing with a vast crater in the center. Trees surround each side, topped with a view of tall mountains. It's a massive space, nestled in the valleys between the mountains we've been climbing all day, and if there was clean Spring water, it would be magnificent.

Unfortunately, the sight before us is anything but. The ground that once held a spring of supposed healing, now holds murky, green colored water that emits a strange odor.

I walk forward in a daze. When I reach the edge of the spring, I look down, hoping it was a trick of distance, wishing to see clean water. But the stinking green substance, growing moss and bacteria, remains. Not a drop of clean spring water in sight.

Reaching my hand out, I attempt to touch the water. A thickly muscled arm blocks my path and shoves me back, causing me to stumble a few steps. I glance at Vlad, a question in my eyes.

He shakes his head. "It smells... dangerous."

With that strange statement, he walks back into the woods. I watch his retreating form disappear from view. He returns a few moments later with a piece of wood. As he nears, it becomes more distinguishable as a sapling ripped from the ground.

Vlad quickly strides back to the edge of the crater. He dips the end of the tree into the dirty water. The instant the wood breaks the surface, a sizzle sounds. The water eats away at the branch like acid.

I gasp, observing Vlad as he carefully lowers the rest of the wood into the water. He's cautious to make sure that none of it splashes towards us as it becomes fully submerged.

Sinking to the ground, I feel defeated. We spent hours traveling here in hopes of a cure, but all we've found is a dead end. I hear a rustling noise from the trees, but I'm too upset to investigate the sound.

Vlad steps closer, his feet entering my range of vision. He doesn't force me up. Instead, he sits and wraps an arm around my shoulder. On my other side, large golden paws appear.

I follow the paws up and find my golden wolf. Our eyes connect and he raises his snout to the air, releasing a howl. The wolves are more disappointed than I am. My golden wolf's howl makes that clear. When it ends, he lies on my other side, resting his head atop his paws.

Still connected to Vlad, I tilt forward and stroke a hand across his fur. He grumbles, but leans into my touch. With a final pat, I tip back and direct my gaze to Vlad. "What do we do now?" I ask.

Vlad opens his mouth to respond, but quickly

snaps it shut. His eyes widen. I hear a snapping noise and whip my head towards the sound.

My golden wolf is shifting and morphing, growing smaller and losing fur. I panic, thinking he's in trouble. Jumping to my feet, I look to Vlad, then Marc a few feet behind us, for help. They're both in shock.

I rush forward, ready to do... something. But when I reach the twisting form on the ground, the golden wolf is gone and in his place is a very naked... Marc? My cheeks heat, and I avert my gaze from his nude form. Meanwhile, my brain goes haywire.

"What is going on?" I force out, my voice shaky. I turn to Marc, clothed Marc, suddenly suspicious. "Leif, is that you again? Is this another trick?"

Marc shakes his head and puts his palms up to pacify me. "No, Mira," He says, his tone low and soothing. "Just give me a second to explain, okay?"

I sigh, confused to the max. But this is Marc, who's helped me, met my family, and done nothing to harm me. At least, not that I know of.

While I think, Vlad growls. My gaze flies to his amber eyes, and I shake my head. His entire body shudders as he inhales deeply, but his growling stops and he nods back.

My eyes return to clothed Marc. "Okay, explain."

He scratches the back of his neck, exchanging a glance with his naked doppelganger. Naked Marc shrugs and clothed Marc sighs.

"This is my brother, Marc. My name is Alex," clothed Marc, err Alex, finally begins. My brow furrows, but I nod, indicating he should continue. He sighs, but explains, "About a year ago, Marc came to Florence to purchase the Daily. Our family has always been interested in documenting history. Everything I told you about my family is true. The only thing I lied about was my name... and owning the Daily." Marc-now-Alex widens his eyes, as if he's trying to convince me of his honesty.

My eyes flit between the brothers, comparing their appearances. "You two are twins?" Marc-now-Alex nods. "Okay, but why are you pretending to be your brother?" I ask, confused.

Alex sighs again. "A few months ago, Marc missed his weekly check-in. It was part of his deal with our parents to leave our... family home. He was, or is required to check-in every weekend. When he missed the following week, I boarded a flight to come find him." He pauses, looking at his brother. His relief is palpable at seeing him in human form. "I arrived at the Daily and someone mistook me for Marc. At that point, I made the decision to pose as my brother while I searched for clues on his whereabouts."

Vlad interjects, "I think I remember this. Marc didn't come to work for almost two weeks, and no one could reach him... When he came back, he said he had a family emergency and flew home. Glenna said she forgot to tell us about Marc reaching out to her, and we all let it go. But for a while, he was off—I can't explain how—he just didn't seem the same."

Marc, no Alex, laughs, his perfect teeth flashing

with the motion. He collects himself and continues, "The first few days were difficult to adjust to. But Glenna was very helpful. She was just as concerned for Marc as I was. Then I found my brother... well, he found me. He appeared in the woods behind his house. We've always had this connection, kind of like the pack. We can communicate with images and a few words. He provided snippets of his memories. The Daily, his normal routines, and how he got stuck as his wolf. He was fighting his wolf's instincts. He had fallen prey to the curse and was trying to break it during his brief bouts of humanity."

"I kept seeing you..." I say to the real Marc. "At the council, the expo, and out in the woods. Then in Vlad's new pack... were you following me?" I ask hesitantly.

The real Marc's emerald gaze connects with mine. He appears shy, offering a slight smile as pink crests his cheeks. He clears his throat twice and his head dips briefly. The movement shows a small glimmer of a scar intersecting his eyebrow. I catalog the difference while waiting for his response.

When he finally speaks, his voice is gravelly, like it's the first time he's spoken in months. According to Alex's story, it very well could be. "I felt, feel, this connection to you. I'm not sure how to explain it." His gaze shifts to the ground near my feet. "For some reason, especially in my wolf form, I feel very protective of you."

"Even though you hadn't met me before?" I ask, perplexed.

"We both felt that way. Well, feel that way," Alex interjects.

I shift my eyes from one twin to the other. Then, I sink back to the ground and place my head between my hands. "What does this all mean?" I ask, lifting my head after a few minutes of thinking.

Vlad wraps his arm around me again. Alex sits on my other side. Marc shuffles a little closer to our group, doing his best to remain modest. The four of us stare at the dirty, murky water.

Marc breaks the silence. "We'll figure this out, Mira. All of it. Now let's try to scrounge together some clothes for my brother and return to camp."

I look at Vlad, then at the identical faces on either side of us. Each of them appears earnest and ready to help. It's not much, but it's a start.

23

THE THREAT

Mirabella

I walk into my kitchen the day after the failed trip to the spring. Both my parents are at the breakfast nook, wearing serious expressions that halt me in my tracks.

"What's going on?" I ask nervously.

My dad silently slides a black envelope towards me, leaving it resting on the edge of the table. His gaze flits from it to me, pointedly. My parents are acting so strangely, dread forms in the pit of my stomach.

I stride to the table to snatch up the envelope. Ripping open an old-school wax seal, I let it fall to the ground and unfold a thick piece of parchment paper. My eyes skim over the words and my brow furrows. I read the parchment three more times before looking at my parents. "A summons from the coven? What is this about?"

Mom and dad exchange a glance. "Mira, honey. You haven't been using any potions in a... malicious way, have you?" My mom asks, hesitantly.

"No." My face pales. "Is that why they sent this? I haven't even been brewing potions. I left my manual at home when Vlad and I went camping!" I exclaim, defending myself against the accusation.

My dad stands and approaches, wrapping me in a brief, warm hug. "We believe you, kiddo. We aren't sure why the Coven sent this. The only way to find out is to respond to the summons."

"Can you come with me?" I ask, nervous by the thought of having to stand in front of a bunch of powerful and important witches by myself.

My parents both solemnly shake their heads, but my mom is the one to answer verbally. "No, honey. You have to do this by yourself. You've done nothing wrong, so everything will be fine."

Glancing back down at the page, I realize the summons is an hour from now. "Oh crap," I mutter. "I need to get ready, so I'm not late."

I rush out of the room without waiting for their response, dashing straight upstairs. I hop in the shower, barely slicking soap off my body before exiting. I yank on my clothes, hoping I can make it on time.

I'm not sure what this summons is for, but I have a feeling the coven won't be thrilled if I'm late.

. . .

I park my Prius, and eye the coven building with trepidation. Before exiting my car, I send a quick text to Vlad: **Received a summons from the coven. I'm not sure what's going on, but I'll message you as soon as I'm out.**

I hold my phone for a few minutes after I hit send, hoping for an immediate reply. When nothing comes, I power down my phone and shove it into the glove box.

Upon reaching the front door of the towering structure, my nerves have almost completely taken over. The knot of dread from earlier remains, sitting low in my belly. My hands are clammy and cold.

Pausing to the side, I wipe them on my jeans. Then I shake out my arms while inhaling a deep breath. Combined, my actions help settle me and I enter the coven building for the second time.

My gaze scans the empty lobby, stopping briefly on the vibrant koi swimming through the pond. I drag my gaze away and briskly stride towards the two ladies at reception. My steps are purposeful and I pull my summons out of my back pocket.

Immediately upon my arrival, one of the women looks up from her tablet. "Mirabella Love?" She asks, a single manicured brow raising up her forehead.

"Yes-s." I stammer out, taken aback.

She makes eye contact, her gaze searching mine before refocusing on her tablet. "You can step to the side. The Head of the Coven will be down to meet you shortly."

My pulse pounds in my head, an insistent staccato formed by fear, but I follow her instructions, stepping to the side of the reception desk. I place the summons back into my pocket, not wanting to ruin it with my clammy hands.

As I wait, I think over every action I've taken since I became a witch. Did they find out about my neighbor's cat? Am I in trouble for being an awful witch?

A pinging noise sounds from the elevators, providing a warning before a woman and two men slip into the lobby. They all wear the black robes standard for the coven, but unlike the other witches I've encountered thus far, they reek of importance.

As they walk closer, I feel the air thicken. It's as if their magic has a physical presence. I want to shrink away from them and their expressionless faces. Forcing myself to stand tall, I ignore the urge to flee. I'm proud that my feet remain firmly planted on the concrete floor as the three imposing figures near.

I look at the female in the center. She appears to be around my grandmother's age, with gray hair pulled into a severe bun resting against her nape. Her lips are puckered as if she's just sucked on a lemon, with several lines surrounding them. The color of her eyes is hidden by half-moon spectacles perched on her small, pert nose.

My gaze scans the males flanking her. Both are around my father's age. One is tall and lean, with dark brown hair and a square jaw. The other is shorter and rounder, with a ruddy complexion and red-orange hair. The trio stops a couple steps away, standing in a straight line with the female in the center, a male on either side.

She runs her eyes over my frame, examining my jeans and fluttery blouse prior to sticking out a weathered hand out. "Esmerelda Fink, Head of the Coven."

Her tone is firm, as is her grip. After our brief handshake, she turns to her left, nodding at the dark-haired man and says, "Paul." Then she moves her head to the right and says, "Ruben." Each of the men gives me a brief nod after she provides their name in lieu of an introduction.

A pause falls over our quartet and I stammer out, "Mira-bell-a." Clearing my throat, I try again. "Mirabella Love."

Esmeralda dips her head in acknowledgement. "We know who you are. Do you know why you're here?"

I decline with a quick shake of my head.

"We have received a summons from the Elder Shifter Council on your behalf. Paul and Ruben are coven attorneys, coming along to represent our interests. We must head there, straightaway."

Without waiting for my response, she twirls on her heel, her robes billowing out in a half-circle with the motion. She marches across the lobby in a diagonal, heading towards a door in the far-left corner. One I hadn't noticed previously. Paul and Ruben walk in sync behind her.

I wait for a beat, then scurry after. While I walk, her words replay on repeat in my mind. Another summons from the Shifter Council?

The climb to the Shifter Council building triggers a sense of déjà vu. Except I'm Vladless this time. As soon as I think his name, I wholeheartedly wish Vlad was with me to address the council again.

Esmerelda interrupts my thoughts as she loudly wraps her knuckles against the massive doors leading into the building. A few seconds later, they creak open, allowing us into the reception area. I file in behind the rest of my party, noting nothing has changed since my last visit.

A man, dressed in what could pass as mountain climbing gear, stands on the far side of the room. As we approach, he motions for us to follow him and winds down a long, windowless hallway.

We walk deep into the building, twisting and turning until we reach a set of familiar doors. He gestures for Esmerelda to open them, stepping to the side and crossing his arms over his expansive chest.

Esmerelda pushes down the handle, then sweeps the door open, allowing it to slam into the wall inside the room. I enter as the tail of the entourage. My gaze fixed straight ahead until we reach the center of the room. I've been in here before and don't need to inspect my surroundings.

As if we'd practiced the movement a hundred

times, the four of us turn in sync to face the Elder Shifter Council seated behind their large, wooden table. My eyes flit across the five figures—four male and one female. The Elders look exponentially more fatigued than the last time I was here. Three of the four sport dark half-circles under their eyes and lightly rumpled clothing, visible signs of their lack of rest.

I examine each of them again, my brow furrowing. The man with graying hair, the one my grandmother referred to as Sylvester, stands to speak, interrupting my inspection. "Ahh, Esmerelda. To what do we owe the *pleasure* of this visit?" His tone is pleasant, but the way the word pleasure rolls off his tongue sounds like he would rather stab himself in the eye with a pencil, then be in the same room as the Head of the Northwestern Coven.

Esmerelda gestures towards me. "You summoned one of our witches. We are here to respond."

Sylvester's eyes widen. "Your witch?" He sputters out.

The three robed figures with me exchange smirks before Esmerelda speaks again, "Yes, she joined the Northwestern Coven recently. As you know, Members of the Coven should not know you exist. But those that do, may not speak to you without the protection of the coven." Her tone is snide, with a hint of superiority.

The Council members appear shocked and Sylvester falls back into his chair. A silence descends upon the room until the singular councilwoman stands and addresses us. "We need to know what progress Mirabella has made. For curing the curse placed on the shifters."

Esmerelda scoffs. "We know of the children's tale you tell your wolves, but there is no curse. Our answer remains the same as it has for years, Rose. The Northwestern Coven will not help the shifters cure the ailment of being unable to effectively govern their own kind. Stop using an alleged curse as an excuse for the actions your rabid wolves take."

With those words, she twirls around, invoking her robe-billowing movement, and striding towards the door. I watch as Ruben and Paul trail behind. Instead of immediately following, I linger, noticing the defeated expressions of the council.

Esmerelda and co. take only a few steps before Sylvester stands again. This time his tone is pleading. "This is bigger than the fate of one small Shifter Community and one Coven, Esmerelda... You know that. As do we."

I drag my eyes from Sylvester to Esmeralda, watching her footsteps falter. The councilman must also see the pause. He hurries to continue his plea. "You can choose to ignore this if you wish, but you know as well as I do, the fate of the Shifters and the Witches are forever bound. We cannot survive without one another. Do you think the witches will continue to exist if all shifters are stripped of their magic? Because we think witches will lose their magic too." Sylvester punctuates his statement with a sweeping motion of his hand, gesturing across the wooden table to encompass himself and the other shifters of the council.

I drift slowly towards the door, towards Esmerelda, wondering how she'll respond to his plight. As I reach the small cluster of witches, she turns from the door and faces the council for the last time. Her expression is unreadable, but her tone is gentler than before. "The Northwestern Coven cannot help you, Sylvester."

Esmerelda pushes back her shoulders and straightens her spine before resuming her exit, followed closely by Ruben and Paul. I take one last, lingering look behind me, watching as Sylvester sinks into his chair. His form slumps forward, his head connecting to his palms resting in front of him. The man to his left rubs a hand down his back in a soothing, circular manner. His lips are moving, but I can't make out the words.

Suddenly, a hand reaches through the open door and grabs my arm in a tight grip, yanking me forward. I stumble to recover, forced to take several quick steps to catch my balance and sync my stride with Esmerelda's. She retraces our path through the Council building at a quick clip.

The three of us reemerge outside. I blink firmly at the shock of the bright summer sun after the dulled fluorescent lights inside. Esmerelda continues to drag me until we've descended the steps into the parking lot.

She abruptly stops and releases me, causing me to

stumble again. She stares at me with a stern expression. "You will tell no one of the shifters." I nod, fearful of the anger present in her eyes. Esmerelda continues, "Above all else, you will never repeat what was said here today. If you do, the Coven cannot and will not protect you."

24

THE REVEAL

Mirabella

The second my butt hits my driver's seat, I pluck my phone from the glove box and power it back on. The screen lights up, then immediately pings with missed messages. I click through each one, reading the concern from my friends and family.

The first name I click is my mom's: **Is all okay? You've been gone a while.**

My fingers fly across the screen as I type up a quick reply: **I'm okay. Was just a congratulatory lunch for passing my exams. I'm heading to Vlad's now.**

I feel a little guilt about lying to her, but I can't tell her the truth. At least not yet and not over text.

Immediately after, I click on Vlad's name next. It's a series of texts starting with: **Call me when you're free.**

Followed by: **I'm getting worried, little Mir.** Then: **Are you okay?**

I respond: **All is okay. Can I come over and talk?**

Vlad's reply is simple and almost immediate: **Yes.**

Next, I click on a message labeled Marc. I make a mental note to change his name in my phone to Alex, as I click the text. **Vlad said the coven summoned you. What is going on??**

With nimble fingers, I reply: **Meet me at Vlad's in 20. Bring your brother.**

I throw my phone down onto the passenger seat, then start my car. With one last glance at the towering coven structure, I back out of the parking lot and head to Vlad's house.

When I pull up to the Mort's house, just over twenty minutes later, Marc's, or maybe Alex's truck is already at the curb. The guys are standing on the porch waiting for me. I park and snatch up my phone, then jog to join them.

Vlad silently opens his front door and we file in the living room. I wait until everyone settles into the couch, then ask, "Are your parents' home?"

Vlad shakes his head. "Nah, they're actually out of town for a few days for their anniversary. They went on a trip to Seattle."

"Okay," I reply, then sigh. Digging into my back pocket, I bring forth the thick piece of parchment paper from the coven and unfold it onto my lap.

"Is that the summons?" Vlad asks. I nod in response and he reaches his hand out. "May I?" I hand the paper to Vlad. He reads it, then passes the simple notice to Marc and Alex. They examine the summons, holding it up to the light like it contains a secret message.

"The words aren't as important as what happened after I went to the coven." I pause, my gaze flitting between the three sets of eyes fixed on me. "When I got there, I met Head of the Coven, Esmerelda Fink. She took me to the Shifter Council, because apparently they summoned me first and the coven intercepted it."

Both Vlad and the real Marc let out low, deep growls at my words.

"I'm okay," I state, not wanting them to transition into massive wolves while I'm trying to relay information. "The coven basically said the council is not allowed to speak to me without their permission and they will never have that permission. Something else was said, though... before Esmerelda dragged me out."

Vlad wraps a comforting arm around me. "You can tell us," he says, urging me to continue.

I glance down at my hands. "I'm not really sure that I understand it exactly. But the Head of the Council pleaded with Esmerelda. He said the fate of the wolves and witches are bound—that one cannot survive without the other. He asked for the coven's help and Esmerelda basically laughed him off, saying the curse was fake. Once we were outside, she told me not to tell anyone about today."

Raising my eyes from my lap, I assess each guy. I start with Vlad, gazing at his furrowed expression as he mulls over the seriousness of the conversation. Next, I examine Alex and he appears to be thinking over all the potential meanings behind her words. I know the real Marc the least, but when my eyes land upon his face, I realize he's very upset over the more obvious implications of the coven's words.

Alex is the first to break the silence. "Maybe the coven wasn't previously aware of the shifters and doesn't know of the curse..."

I appreciate his willingness to see the best in people and the best in the actions of the coven, but I disagree. "She knew Sylvester's name," I point out. "And they made it sound like the wolves' curse is used as an excuse for wolves that misbehave. It's obvious they know of the curse and the wolves," I finish.

The four of us fall into another silence, thinking over what this additional information could mean for the curse and for the shifters.

"What do we do now?" Vlad finally asks.

"I think we need to gather witches we trust and tell them about the shifters. We're going to need extra help if the coven plans to ignore the curse... and I need to go to the Canadian coven to find answers."

"Mira's right," Marc says, surprising me with his immediate support. "Even if the coven won't step in, the support of other witches may be enough. If we all go to the Canadian coven together, we might convince them to assist us. The Northwestern coven won't matter then."

Before we can discuss our ideas further, a knock sounds at the Mort's front door. I glance at Vlad. He shrugs and rises from the couch to answer it. He only opens the door partway, but we can still hear muffled words from the other side.

"Vladimir Mort, you are being summoned by the council." The speaker shoves against Vlad and he stumbles backwards, widening the opening of the door. "Alexander Sieves and Marcus Sieves, you are also being summoned to the council."

"Okay," Vlad replies calmly. "When do we need to be there?"

"Right now. I'm here to take you in," the man states.

Vlad looks back at me with wide eyes.

I mouth, "What should I do?"

Vlad casually states, "Well Alex and Marc, it looks like we're going to be tied up for a while. Mira, why don't you get started on our plans? The three of us will join you as soon as we can."

WITHIN AN HOUR, I'm able to gather my grandma, the Amica's minus Sylvia's younger brothers, and my parents. The six of them wait patiently, scattered around the living room. I pace in a line across the front, trying to organize my thoughts enough to explain.

"Is everything okay?" My mom asks, sounding

concerned after my twentieth time walking the length of the room.

I stop pacing and face the group spread across my parent's couches. "No."

My dad jumps off the couch and rushes towards me. I put my hands up to stop him and motion for him to sit back down.

Sighing, I correct myself. "Everything is okay with me, I mean. But I have something to tell you, and I need to ask for your help." I look each person in the eye, before continuing, "I'm going to reveal a secret today. The information you hear in this room cannot be repeated outside of these walls. I need you to promise that you'll keep an open mind until I finish explaining."

The adults exchange an indiscernible glance. I give them a couple of minutes to make up their minds. Eventually everyone's gaze returns to the front. To my surprise, Sylvia's dad speaks for the group. "We will listen to what you have to say. Then determine if we can help afterwards."

I nod. "That's fair. Uhm, I don't really know where to start..." I inhale a deep breath and begin, "A few months ago, I discovered that shifters exist and an entire pack lives in Florence."

A gasp interrupts me, but I push forward, knowing I need to tell the story first and address questions later. "A wolf shifted into a boy right before my eyes. After that, an Elder Shifter Council summoned me for questioning. They told me of a curse affecting the shifters. It causes them to lose their humanity. The council wanted to hold me captive, thinking I knew of the cure. But I was saved by grandma, which is how we met."

"Recently, the coven revealed that they don't want witches to know shifters exist." I look at my parents, eyeing their inscrutable expressions. "The summons I received earlier today, from the coven... was on behalf of the Shifter Council. Esmerelda and two attorneys brought me to the council and told the wolves their curse was fake. After we left, Esmerelda demanded I keep all this a secret."

"Then why are you telling us?" Sylvia's mom asks.

Her question is valid. "I... we... the shifters and I need your help. I've been seeking a cure for the curse, but I've hit a dead end. I think I need to travel to the Canadian coven. They might have the answers I'm searching for, or be able to point me in the right direction. But while I'm gone, someone in Florence has to continue our search."

My eyes sweep the room again. The group's faces are unreadable, so I continue, "I'm not positive, but I think shifters and witches are connected. If we can cure the shifters, we might be able to access the rest of our magic. Like magic beyond potion brewing."

For the first time in my entire life, well that I can remember, my parents don't immediately offer their support. My mom and dad silently communicate before meeting my gaze.

"Mira," my mom begins, her tone a juxtaposition of

hesitant but firm. "We love you and we want to help you grow in any way we can... but I think we need to speak with the coven first to get their opinion about something of this magnitude. If the shifters exist and there is a curse affecting everyone, the coven should know about it. I'm sure if they already know, they're working on a cure."

I'm shocked by her words. "IF shifters exist? IF a curse exists?" The disbelief in my tone is palpable. Out of every reaction I prepared for, a lack of support wasn't one that had crossed my mind. "Mom, half our town is shifters. Vlad is a shifter. Most of our magic is gone. These are irrefutable facts. The coven told me today they will not help with anything involving the shifters."

"Mira." My mom sighs, as if she's exasperated by this conversation.

"No, mom. I'm not finished." I cut her off, which isn't the norm for me.

I'm not usually an angsty teenager that fights against her parents. I don't know that I've ever had a serious argument with them, but this is something I'm willing to fight for. The stakes are too high to meekly fall into line at the smallest hint of resistance.

"Whether you choose to see it or not, our fate is bound to the fate of the shifters. I believe that wholeheartedly and I don't know why you don't trust me. If you take this to the coven... I'm not sure how they'll punish me."

My dad addresses my grandmother, ignoring my

passionate statement. "Molly, did you put her up to this?"

"No, Arthur," she responds firmly. "No one 'put her up to this'. Mira is telling you the truth and you need to choose whether you listen. I hope you do, but I can't make that choice for any of you." Her gaze sweeps across the room pointedly.

The parents exchange looks again, then rise as a single unit from the couch. Sylvia's dad is the only one that meets my eyes. "We won't bring this to the coven, but we can't offer you support for something without proof of its existence."

The four of them file out of the room, leaving only Sylvia, my grandma, and myself behind. Sylvia has said nothing, but once the adults exit, she chimes in. "Is this why you were acting so strange as the beginning of the summer? And why you were always with Vlad?"

"Yes."

I'm nervous Sylvia's upset over this secret I've been keeping for the past few months. I create a list of reasons I didn't tell her before now, especially after the whole witch-secret issue. I ready my defense against the accusations I expect.

A short "hmm" leaves her lips. I remain at the front of the room, compiling reasons for my secrecy. "I believe you," she finally says, to my disbelief.

"You do?" I ask.

She nods her head. "Of course, I do. Why would you lie about something like this?"

I shrug, at a loss for words. I don't deserve a friend like Sylvia.

"I want to help. What's next?"

25

THE PORTAL

Mirabella

After she gets home from the disastrous meeting with our parents, Sylvia starts a group chat in the new messenger app we downloaded. Somehow, she already acquired Alex and Marc's phone number. I don't ask her methods, she's just resourceful like that.

Sylvia titles the new group "Canada Crew" and sends out a barrage of messages.

BA Witch S: **Hey, is it cold in Canada in the summer? Should I pack cold weather gear?**

Wolf Boy: **Why don't you use your phone and check the weather app?**

I read her first text and Vlad's response, then put my phone down with a chuckle. Apparently, the person who starts the chat can choose names for each person in the group. As I continue to pack, my phone blows up with messages. I leave the dinging to continue while I flip through the hangers in my closet.

BA Witch S: **I didn't have the zip code to look it up.**

Fake Marc: **I would bring, at the very least, one pair of jeans and one sweater. The evenings may get colder in Canada than they have been here. The days will probably be warmer than the nights.**

Fake Marc: **Why can't I be in the group text as Alex? ... Since it's my name.**

BA Witch S: **You faked being a man named Marc for months and now it's URGENT we call you Alex? Okay.**

Marc: **HAHAHAHA**

When I finally finish packing enough outfits for a week or so, I read through the messages. I roll my eyes at Sylvia's antics before adding a message for the group.

BA Witch M: **Let's meet at my grandmother's house in an hour.**

Responses flood in, but I ignore them, and inspect my room a final time. I want to ensure I don't forget anything important for our trip to the Canadian coven. Suddenly remembering my witching texts, I reach into my closet to grab the book from my birthday. Then I add the three books from Leif into my duffel bag.

I rush out of my room, to the bookcase hiding my parent's witching chamber. Carefully plucking my way down the steps, I dash straight to a shelf of books. I grab the legacy book that Leif showed me, then a potions manual, just in case. Bringing my haul back upstairs, I dump them into my duffel.

As I'm tugging the zipper closed, a slightly out of breath Jacob appears in my doorway. "Miss Love," he whispers in an urgent tone.

I abandon my duffel to face him, concerned by his tone. "What's going on, Jacob?"

"Miss Love," he repeats, then shifts his eyes to the hall behind him. "We need to get you out of here, right away. Esmerelda Fink and others from the coven are downstairs in the kitchen with your parents. They're delaying them for as long as possible, but we don't have much time."

"Esmerelda Fink?" I ask, my brain slow to interpret his words. "What is she doing here?"

"They're here for you. Somehow she found out you shared the information about the Shifters and the Council." Jacob steps through my open door and yanks the zipper on my duffle. Once it's closed, he places it over his shoulder, then puts a firm, but gentle, hand against my back. He steers me towards the stairs. "Go out the back and run to your car. Drive to Molly's as quickly as you can. She'll know what to do."

He leads me to the door and quietly slides it open, handing me my bag with a nod. I follow his instructions, sprinting to my car. Jumping in, I immediately start my Prius and back down the driveway while using one of my hands to jab at my Stereo.

A call rings out once, then Sylvia's voice comes through my speakers. "Hello."

"I need you to come outside immediately," I say frantically, spotting my parent's door open and Esmerelda's stormy face peering outside. "Plans changed. I'm picking you up right now. We need to head to my grandma's, quickly. Tell the others."

SYLVIA REACHES in front of her to place a hand against the dash, emitting a "eek." I whip my car into the empty spot next to the Sieves brothers' truck. We both hurry to pull our luggage out of the backseat and sprint to my grandmother's red door. It opens the second my foot hits the bottom step, my grandma's gray hair peeking out.

A look of relief crosses her face and she ushers us forward. "The boys are already inside, hurry dearies."

The door firmly shuts behind Sylvia and I. My gaze focuses on the couches in the living room where Alex, Marc, and Vlad are already waiting for us. Vlad rises to his feet, taking in my flushed and panicked appearance, and releases an angry growl.

He strides across the room in three steps and yanks me against him. His thick arms cross my back, holding me tightly against his broad form. I feel his inhale as he buries his face into my hair and breaths. Something about my scent reassures him and he loosens his hold incrementally.

"What happened?" He asks, his voice rumbling through me.

His hold, and the fact that my crew is safe, has the

tension slowly draining from my body. "Esmerelda Fink, Head of the Coven, is after me. She came to my house."

"What did she want?" Marc, or maybe Alex, asks.

"She found out I shared information about the shifters after she told me not to," I reply, muffled by Vlad's chest.

My grandma gasps, but it's Sylvia that voices the thought that's been running through my head since Jacob helped me escape. "Who told her? How did she find out?"

"I'm not sure," I reply hesitantly.

I don't want to suspect anyone close to me, but those are the only people I've talked to since the summons. I step back, out of Vlad's hold, and push the thoughts of betrayal to the back of mind.

Instead, I address a more pressing matter, "How can we leave Florence? We haven't even made travel plans yet."

I scan the room until I land on my grandma's twinkling eyes. "You'll use magic, of course." She walks through the living room, pausing in the doorway to the kitchen. I widen my stance, settling in for the lengthy explanation I know will come next.

She shocks me by not explaining further. She motions us to follow her, then continues towards the back of the house. The five of us stare after her until she calls, "Come, come".

The words spur our group into motion. Making our way through the house, we follow her down a hallway of closed doors. She opens the last door on the right and steps inside. The five of us file in behind her.

The room is devoid of windows and completely bare, except for an empty door frame sitting in the exact middle of the space.

"What is this?" I ask quizzically, after my brief inspection.

"This is a portal, dear," my grandmother replies, like this should be obvious.

"A portal?" Sylvia asks, her voice sounding reverent. She sounds like she's heard the word before and it's something to admire.

Vlad looks from my grandma, to Sylvia, then to the empty frame, like he's missed something. After a few beats, he asks, "What does it do?"

Mentally, I second his question and wonder if Alex and Marc have ever heard of a portal before.

My grandmother pulls a vial of black liquid from her ruby colored robes and steps forward. She upturns the vial and pours its contents on the floor, directly underneath the doorless door frame. The second the liquid touches the floor, she murmurs a string of words too low to hear.

I watch in wonder as the once empty frame fills with a shimmery silver substance. It creates a semi-sheer element that looks like a cross between water and gas. The silvery shimmer completes the door within the frame and fluctuates in random, swirling patterns as if it's a living creation.

With the frame full, my grandma turns back to the

group. "You'll each step through the portal and it will transport you to the Canadian coven."

My eyes widen, and I step closer to examine the portal. It continues to move, shimmering in the light from the ceiling. "Why didn't you use this to travel to the Canadian coven before?" I ask, recalling how my grandma drove when she went to ask for help on the town's behalf.

"It was on the fritz," my grandma replies. "Leif fixed it for me while he was staying here. He said it was the least he could do to repay my hospitality. He's a very kind and helpful young man," she finishes with a small smile.

"What if he sabotaged it?" Sylvia questions in a low tone, her eyes meeting mine.

I have the same fear, but I don't voice the words aloud.

"We don't have any other options. All we can do is hope that he didn't," I respond with the truth. "I will do everything in my power to cure this curse, but if you're not sure you want to commit, I won't be upset if you don't accompany me." I meet the eyes of each person present, then step through the portal.

26

THE CITY

Mirabella

My grandma didn't prepare us for the landing. At all. A tangle of limbs and bags, the five of us hit the cobbled ground, hard, landing in a massive heap. I groan as someone's backpack nails me in the gut the same second my hip hits the ground.

"Shouldn't the portal contain a spell for a gentle landing?" I mutter, attempting to untangle myself enough to stand.

"Maybe we should've drunken float potions before we jumped through," Alex's voice groans back, slightly muffled.

Looking to my side, I see Alex is half under Sylvia, her abdomen covering his head. She's splayed out like she's pretending to be Superman flying through the air, and the tips of her fingers are touching Vlad's calves.

Vlad is half on a suitcase, and under two duffle bags. Marc is right next to him, their hips touching and a backpack slightly overlapping their bellies. Strangely, I landed by myself a few feet away, instead of inside the pile my friends and our luggage created.

Despite the twinge of pain from our landing, I chuckle. I half sit-up, resting on my elbows to inspect our rag-tag group after our awful landing. A chorus of light groans meets my amused chuckle, and I force myself the rest of the way up.

Stepping over to the group, I offer my hand first to Sylvia, lifting her off Alex. From there we help the others up. Once finished, I stretch my tender muscles and right my luggage.

A whirring noise catches my attention and I raise my gaze to the sky in time to see a teenager floating through the air above our heads. His feet are planted firmly, hip-width apart, on a shimmery blue disc. My eyes widen at the sight and I point out the kid to the rest of the group.

"What is that?" Vlad asks, his voice rumbling in a quiet half-whisper.

"I don't know," I whisper back.

"This place is insane," Sylvia states, quietly.

The five of us spin in a circle, silently absorbing our surroundings. Tall, thin, pink buildings glisten in the hazy sun, as if they're made of gems. We appear to be surrounded by shops, but the writing on the signs is strange. It's made of squiggly lines that don't appear to be letters. I squeeze my eyes shut then reopen them, hoping to bring the markings into focus.

It doesn't work.

Shaking my head, I continue examining the area, noting the cobbled road, and the paved sidewalks filled with people. Some of them eye our group curiously, but no one approaches us. Their reactions make me wonder if groups of people and baggage falling out of the sky and landing on this part of the road are a frequent occurrence.

Out of the corner of my eye, I see Alex lean over and poke at the cobbled road with a single finger. He straightens up and then looks towards the pink structures.

"What is this place?" Sylvia whispers, in a tone tinged with awe.

My eyes do another sweep of our surroundings, noting the impressive pink buildings, pausing on a castle-like structure directly down the road. Somehow, I hadn't noticed it previously, despite the tall, white, skinny turrets extending high into the air, differentiating it from the others nearby.

Dragging my eyes away from the mysterious building, I continue my sweep of the area. My eyebrows raise at a sign written in an old English style font. "It looks like it's a witching city called 'Haven'," I respond in a hushed tone, pointing to the sign off to the side.

As a group, we wordlessly wander towards the sign, dragging our luggage along behind us. Stopping directly in front of the slightly weathered wood, our eyes scan the words. "Haven. The City of Witches. All are welcome here."

Underneath the words is a counter that appears to be fluctuating as people fly in and out of the town on their floating blue discs. It finally registers that the number is a counter reflecting the number of people in the city. While staring at the sign, the number has hovered steadily around five-thousand.

Five-thousand witches. All in one place. I'm in awe of how large this city must actually be. I turn my head towards Vlad, but I'm interrupted before I'm able to form words.

"Ahh, Mira Love," a voice calls from behind us. I recognize the slightly accented tone, having heard it often over the past months. They belong to someone I was hoping to avoid during this trip, as unlikely as it seemed. The voice continues, "I wasn't expecting to see you again, so soon."

As a unit, the five of us turn from the sign to face the city once more. Standing on the street before us is a small crowd of witches, some clad in robes, and others dressed more casually. Three figures stand in a line, slightly ahead of the rest.

In the center is a distinguished man with light brown hair and piercing blue eyes, in a set of black robes. I immediately recognize his face from my Foogle searches, however, he doesn't hold my attention.

My eyes flit to his right, to a willowy girl with flowing blonde hair and Archibald's piercing blue eyes.

She gives me a look that I assume is a smile, but looks more like she's baring her teeth at me.

My eyes drift to the left. It's there that I finally spot the owner of the voice.

"Leif," I say simply.

To be continued...

(Keep reading for a sneak peek at Shattered The Curse Trilogy Book 3, available now on Amazon!)

SNEAK PEEK

SHATTERED: THE CURSE TRILOGY BOOK 3

Mirabella

I'll escort you to your quarters," Archibald Golden states, after we've established the reason for our small crews' arrival.

"Err... that's okay. I'm sure someone, literally anyone else, could escort us. You probably have more important things to do than show us to our accommodations," I protest, not wanting to spend any more time in Coven Leader Golden's presence. The last few hours of questioning in a giant conference room were more than enough already.

"No, no, I insist," Mr. Golden states, waving his hand in the air as if he's brushing my worries aside like a pesky fly.

"Really, we're fine," I protest again, feebly.

"Ahh, I just need to think of a building that has five empty rooms," he mutters, pivoting on his heel and stepping a few feet away while he thinks.

"We could double up in rooms, it's no trouble. We just appreciate the ability to use your archives and your willingness to host us with such limited notice," Marc interjects, shooting a beaming smile at Mr. Golden.

I look at Marc, trying to convey gratitude with my

eyes. He shoots me a quizzical look, so I'm not quite sure that the expression sent the appropriate message.

"Absolutely not," Mr. Golden responds adamantly. "My coven would never cram visitors into one room, we have plenty of space, especially for such esteemed guests. In fact, I have just the place, although it is a bit of a trek. It will give you the chance to see the city, however."

"Sounds great," Marc replies, halfheartedly. A beaming smile still sits across his lips; however, the expression doesn't quite reach his eyes.

My gaze scans Vlad, Alex, and Sylvia. It's obvious that everyone is barely holding it together. Following the stress of our rapid escape from Florence through the portal, then the hours of questioning we endured following our arrival, it isn't too surprising, but I wish there was a way to hurry Mr. Golden.

He finally moves to the door, holding it open and beckoning for us to follow. I want to groan in relief at the thought of collapsing into a bed, but thankfully I'm able to contain the sound, barely.

Mr. Golden leads us out of the pink crystal building in a winding path and eventually we emerge onto the cobbled streets of Haven. The road seems like it's for pedestrian use only, as hover discs fill the air space above, transporting witches between buildings and out of the city.

Tearing my gaze away from the sky, I glance at the shops lining the cobbled road. Once we were accepted into the town by the coven, a spell seemed to lift. All the words on the signs that appeared to be gibberish are suddenly legible.

Mr. Golden marches us past the "Ingredient Shop", "Witches Brewery", and "Witch Cream" shops. I stare intently into each window, wondering if we'll have an opportunity to come back this way soon.

I'm torn from my thoughts when I suddenly slam into a solid wall of rock-hard muscle. Bouncing off upon impact, I immediately hit the hard cobblestone for the second time today and emit an "oomph".

Looking up, I spot Alex, who came to a dead stop in the middle of the road for no reason. He twirls around, his expression turning panicked until he spots me sprawled rather ungracefully across the hard ground. "Oh, shit Mira, sorry." He offers his hand to help me up, but no other explanation.

I place my palm into his, using the grip to assist me to my feet. Instead of releasing me, Alex intertwines our fingers and slows his pace so we're able to walk side by side. He leads me a few feet away to join the rest of the group clustering at the entrance of a tall, pink building nearby.

Forgetting our hands are connected, I pause at the edge of our crew. My gaze floats over the cylindrical bottom of the tower, drifting upwards until I'm forced to crane my neck. The building stretches for what seems like miles, ending in the sky at a thin, pointed top.

I scan the surrounding area and spot the large, pink castle-like structure just to the left of the building.

To the right is an empty expanse. Some distance away sits another building comprised of the crystalline material, only this one starts with a square base, graduating into a thin rectangle as it reaches for the clouds.

My mystified eyes finally connect with Mr. Golden's and he nods his head once, as if he was waiting to regain my attention. "This is Guest Building H," he announces, opening his arms wide to encompass the building in front of us. "You will live here for the duration of your stay in Haven."

"It's a very nice building, sir. Everything in Haven is spectacular," Sylvia chimes in with a sickly, sweet smile.

Mr. Golden returns the look with one more genuine, apparently unable to discern Sylvia's face lacks any genuine happiness. "I'm so glad you're already enjoying your time here. Come, come. I'll show the highlights of the building, then lead you to your rooms to retire. I'm sure you are all very exhausted from your journey."

Maybe he's not as oblivious as I originally thought.

The five of us trail into the building behind Mr. Golden like a gaggle of ducklings. We stop shortly after passing through a double set of doors made of a cloudy, crystal substance. "This is the Lobby," Mr. Golden states and I stifle a groan. If this is what he calls a 'highlight' it's going to take eight years for us to reach our rooms.

<u>To be continued...</u>

INTERESTED IN NEWS ABOUT BOOKS BY NICOLE MARSH?

Check out her socials here!

INTERESTED IN NEWS ABOUT BOOKS BY CASSY JAMES?

Check out her socials here!

BOOKS BY NICOLE MARSH

The Curse Trilogy (Paranormal Romance)

Cursed

Bound

Shattered

Standalone

The Con

BOOKS BY CASSY JAMES

The Curse Trilogy (Paranormal Romance)

Cursed

Bound

Shattered

Rockin' Love Duet

Electric Wounds

Intoxicating Hearts

Made in United States
Cleveland, OH
05 September 2025